SHIFTED IN SEATTLE

Lisa Medley

Cover and formatting by Sweet 'N Spicy Designs

Published in the United States of America

Lisa Medley

http://www.lisa-medley.com

Chapter One

The most merciful thing in the world, I think, is the inability of the human mind to correlate all its contents. We live on a placid island of ignorance in the midst of a black sea of infinity, and it was not meant that we should voyage far. – The Call of Cthulhu by H.P. Lovecraft

"Ruby! It's him!"

Ruby Parsons peered around her iPad at her roommate Claire, who bounced excitedly on the opposite end of the couch. "And who would *he* be?"

"Listen to this *Daveslist* "Near Misses" ad:

H.P. Lovecraft: Stand-Up Comedian – m4w (Annex Theater) - Seattle

Tuesday night, after the show, you and I flirted while in line for the bathroom. We agreed that even if the staff had to clean up a blood sacrifice, the place was still nicer than the streets below.

You smiled at me as you took off, but there was no chance for me to get your name.

Buy you a drink sometime? We might as well enjoy ourselves before Cthulhu rises…"

Ruby scrambled across the couch and stuffed herself into the crack between Claire and the cushioned back for a look at the ad.

"It's Cthulhu! Your Lovecraftian lobster," Claire said, handing over the iPad for her to see.

"You have got to quit watching *Friends* reruns." Ruby read the ad. Her heart hammered in her chest, and a blush of heat covered her face and neck. It was him. Too many exact details not to be. Still. A classified ad? In "Near Misses"? It was so…seedy. Wasn't it? What kind of people posted ads like that, or worse…responded to them? "Listen, I met the guy for like thirty seconds in line for the bathroom."

"And then reread *The Call of Cthulhu* even though you practically have the thing memorized and went on and on and on about him and his hipster beardedness for weeks. Weeks!" Claire snatched her iPad out of Ruby's hands then launched off the couch and into the swinging papasan chair. She began typing furiously on the tablet.

"What are you doing?" Ruby asked, concerned.

"Answering him, of course."

"No!" Ruby raced across the tiny apartment to try to retrieve the iPad before the damage could be done, but Claire gave the chair a hard spin and kept typing. "Stop! Seriously, what if he's a serial killer?"

"He's not a serial killer. He likes comedians. And *reads*. Serial killers don't do either of those things."

"You don't know that. Claire—"

"Done!" Claire extended a foot from the Tilt-A-Whirl and anchored herself to the floor. The chair came to an abrupt stop then twisted around the opposite direction, uncoiling.

Ruby snatched the iPad from her roommate's hands before Claire could get her bearings and read the screen: *Yes! I can't believe you found me. Would LOVE to meet you for coffee, a drink, a show...whatever!*

Ruby sighed. At least Claire had logged in under her own *Daveslist* account and not Ruby's. Not that it really mattered. This was Seattle. Every other twenty-something guy with a beard in town was a software engineer or a hacker it seemed. Nothing digital was sacred anymore.

God. What if he replies?

"I can't believe you did that." Ruby handed back the tablet and sank to the floor, half-scared but half-excited. She'd never have had the guts to reply herself. Growing up in the Midwest, she'd still not shed her childhood lessons, long instilled by her farmer parents.

Don't talk to strangers was probably number one. *Don't talk to strange men on the Internet* was definitely a close second. Moving to the very liberal city of Seattle for college and then going to work for Google didn't mean she'd thrown all of her morals and teaching out the windows, however.

Claire, on the other hand…

The iPad chirped with a notification. They both jumped then raced to see.

Friday night? The Annex? Weird and Awesome *show? Seemed fitting. Since finding you there...and now here is both Weird and AWESOME! Say yes. I'll be there. Waiting for you. In the front row. All hopeful-like. I'm not a serial killer.*

Claire's eyebrows nearly leaped off her face in her glorious satisfaction. "I. Told. You. So! Not a serial killer!"

Ruby rolled her eyes; her heart stampeded in her chest now. "Of course he'd say that. They all say that."

Oh God. Oh God. Oh God.

"I've never seen that show. Have you?" Claire asked, her voice echoing down the long hallway of Ruby's consciousness as she tried to hear her over the crashing surf of blood pounding in her ears.

"You're going to go, right? I mean. What are the chances? First of him placing an ad to find you. Of us seeing the ad and of him responding so quickly? It's meant to be, Ruby. Seriously, this is cosmic karma or something. Yeah. You're totally going." Claire waved a hand in Ruby's face, snapping her back to the room. "Right?"

"I…it's…what if…"

"Stop right there. If you don't meet him and at least give this guy a chance, you'll never forgive yourself. Here's a what-if for you. What if he's THE ONE? What if he's your one and only chance at love, and you let him pass by not once but twice? Most people don't get a second chance, Ruby. Hell, I'm still waiting for a first chance. If you don't go, I will."

"You don't even know Lovecraft!"

"Nope, but I can fake it. Heck, I might even read one of those stories. A short one. A really short one. How long are those stories anyway? That looks like a pretty thick book."

Ruby followed Claire's gaze to the bookshelf then made haste to grab the volume before it fell into the wrong hands.

"No need. I'll go." Ruby swallowed hard around the painful lump of anxiety growing in her throat.

"Yay! And whew! I was worried there for a minute. I mean, I haven't cracked open a book since college."

"Yeah. That's what you should be worried about, being forced to read. Good luck finding another roommate after they discover my dismembered body in the Sound."

"You don't think I'd let you go alone, do you? I'm sure I can scrounge up someone to go with me. We'll sit in the back. Throw popcorn at your head. Bail you out if things seem to be going horribly wrong."

"That would be the least you could do." Ruby ran her hand across the leather book cover of *H.P. Lovecraft: The Complete Fiction*. "I'm going to go read."

"Alrighty then, homework it is! Good night, Ruby. And yes, I'll be maid of honor at your wedding. You won't regret this."

"Famous last words."

***

Ethan Lane couldn't believe his luck. He paced the floor of his Arts and Crafts style living room and looked out onto the Sound. Not only had she seen his lame ad, but she'd responded. He'd never placed a "Near Misses" ad. Ever. But he couldn't get the cute brunette off his mind. Being a writer in Seattle was so cliché, it was painful sometimes and lonely. He couldn't contain his literary geekiness, and when he'd seen the flyer for the Lovecraft comedy show? He'd buy that ticket all day, every day. He hadn't been able to talk any of his friends into going to the show, so he'd gone alone and met Ruby. One more gin and tonic, and he'd have gotten her number. Of course, too many more gin and tonics and he'd have had to take a cab instead of driving himself all the way across town, over the ferry and home to Bainbridge. What a mess that would have become. On a full moon, no less. He'd been right to forgo the liquid courage. *Drink Responsibly* and all that.

Remembering that night brought a smile to his face. He watched the surf pound against the shore below. He was a lucky, lucky man. His writing had made him quite successful. Rather, his pen name, Robin Woodring, was successful. If his people knew how he was really making his living, he'd be disowned or worse. While his writing hadn't exactly been a secret, his accomplishment had. They all assumed he was a day trader and his writing was a quirky hobby. He tipped a tumbler of bourbon to his lips and let the amber liquid slide on in. His mind scrambled through the jumble of possibilities and potential pitfalls of what he'd done. He wondered if she'd show up Friday. Her reply seemed jubilant enough and hopeful.

His insides twisted.

She'd gotten all of his juvenile Lovecraft jokes in the three or four minutes they'd waited outside the only theater bathroom for the previous occupant to vacate. Finally, she'd gone in and while he waited his turn outside the door, trying to find some witty, non-creepy way to ask for her number, he'd lost his nerve. Or more, his sanity had returned. There was a reason shifters didn't date the normals.

Actually, there were *a lot* of reasons.

God, he was playing with fire. He scratched at his beard. He shaved daily, yet by this time every day he sported a beard that would take six months for a normal to grow. Sometimes he trimmed it during the day. Luckily, Seattle was a big city, and he could usually spread his service needs around so he didn't see the same vendors twice in one day, causing them to wonder why he'd been clean-shaven for the morning meeting and looked like Teen Wolf by five o'clock drinks. Not a problem with the clan, but it made it nearly impossible to maintain outside friendships, let alone a relationship. He shuddered.

What the hell was he thinking? He'd met her late, so beard it would have to be, to make sure she recognized him. But then what? Luckily, the problem was contained to his face. Unless he let it go too long then it became a problem…everywhere. And quickly. If he didn't shave every day, his face and chest would be full-on Sasquatch by the end of the week. And the moon! God, the full moon would only hasten the effect.

Sweat began to bead along his spine and lower back. He paced faster.

He could cancel. Just not show up Friday night. She didn't know his name. Or anything about him. There was no way for her to track him down. This was stupid. Hazardous. Reckless.

But the optimism swirling around his heart called it something else…hope.

None of the females of his clan had lit up that spark of hope in him like she had in the few minutes he'd spent with her. What if she was the one?

The One!

The cycle could be broken. He could be normal. Well, more normal. And the shifting would be limited.

Shifting once a month and freedom from daily shaving would be life changing. Or so he'd been told. Only a few had actually broken free of their nature. And were promptly excommunicated for their efforts.

The shift suppression shots he took each month helped, but they weren't foolproof. Mating with a normal would mean their children wouldn't carry the gene to initiate the magic necessary for the shift. And it was some sort of magic. An ancient magic remembered and recorded by shamans around the globe.

The only way Sasquatches could procreate was to, well, procreate while in their Sasquatch form. And the females? They had to stay in Sasquatch form for the nine months it took to gestate. It was brutal. Most of the males stayed with the females to protect them during that time. It was a dangerous and terrifying ordeal for Sasquatch families. And one he didn't have any plans to propagate. He wasn't ashamed of his heritage, but, in the twenty-first century, with a security camera on every corner and a cell phone in every hand, living as a Sasquatch was becoming riskier.

It was only a matter of time before they were outed once and for all. His clan had lived in the Pacific Northwest for centuries. The Lummi Indians called them *Ts'mekwes* and had helped them to keep their secret for uncountable moons. They were practically rock stars on the reservation, and many of them lived there. Hell, *most* of them lived there or across the border in Canada. Others returned for solace or when the moon called them. So far, any indiscretions had been covered up, glossed over, or worked into cable documentaries no one really took seriously except the die-hard hunters. The clan scanned the Bigfoot Field Department's online boards and sighting reports with a fine-tooth comb, searching for infractions of clan members near and far and making sure to discount any actual sightings. It didn't take much to turn a confirmation into a hoax. Still, some of the Bigfoot Field Department faithful were getting craftier. For the most part, everyone agreed, those BFD people were crazy.

Nearly as crazy as he was for trying this, but he longed for a normal life.

Yeah, playing with fire.

And nothing stinks more than a burning Sasquatch.

Chapter Two

Ruby finished the last paragraph of *The Call of Cthulhu* on her phone then reread it once more. She'd reread it each of the past three nights like she was cramming for finals. One passage stood out to her. "Who knows the end? What has risen may sink, and what has sunk may rise. Loathsomeness waits and dreams in the deep and decay spreads over the tottering cities of men."

Right. The perfect romance-inspiring fiction to bond over. Clearly, they were a match made in Heaven.

Crap.

"Quit making that face," Claire said, pulling up to the curb in front of the theater.

"I can't. I'm nervous."

"Then let me come with you, like I promised."

Ruby shook her head then stuffed her phone into her tiny purse. "No. I can do this. It's a public place. Look, there's a line already. I'll be fine."

"At intermission, you go to the bathroom and text me an update. I want to know how it's going. Text me again at eleven, when it's over. I'll come get you then or, if you want to go out for drinks or something, I'll pick you up there. Do not get into a car with him, though. Do you understand?"

Ruby sighed. "Now you're concerned?"

"Cautiously optimistic and 78 percent sure he's not a serial killer."

"That's a much lower percentage than you stated earlier. You're not helping."

"I'm kidding." Claire unlocked the car doors. "Promise about the texting. I'm fifteen minutes away. Don't make me put your face on a milk carton. I'll use the one I took after you pulled your stocking cap off after skiing at Snoqualmie."

"That's low."

"These are serious times. The stakes are high."

Ruby sucked in a deep breath through her nose and blew it out of her mouth. "Okay. I'm on it."

Claire pulled her in for a quick hug. "I hope he turns out to be a prince."

"I'd have to kiss him to find out."

"True. No kissing. We'll Google-stalk him later. A name. At least get a name this time."

"Thanks. I'll see you soon." Ruby opened the door and stepped onto the sidewalk, glad she'd bought her ticket early. Judging from the line, *Weird and Awesome* was popular. Who knew?

Terror and excitement battled within her in an intestinal tug-o-war as she fished her ticket out of her pocket. Bypassing the purchase line, she walked to the entrance door and handed the paper to the staff member.

"Enjoy the show." He took her ticket, and she went inside.

The theater buzzed with conversation, and her stomach filled with butterflies as she scanned down the rows to the front. While she had no idea what he looked like from behind, her options were rather limited. Only one open front row seat remained. She walked forward, her feet heavy and her legs weak. She wished she'd arrived first. Saved him the seat. Let him be the anxious one.

As she contemplated backing up the aisle and texting Claire from the bathroom to retrieve her, a man in the front row turned around and looked up the aisle at her. Squinting into the spotlight, he covered his brow with his hand to shield his eyes. He probably couldn't even really see her. But she could see him fine. He was just as sexy as she remembered. His reddish-brown beard seemed a bit fuller maybe. It was hard to know. Three minutes wasn't long enough to memorize the exactness of his facial hair. Although, she could definitely describe him to a police sketch artist if necessary.

Still not too late. *Bolt! Run! Go home and read!*

And then he waved. And stood up. All six-sixish of him.

The smile spreading across his face between his mustache and that rugged beard was adorable and wicked. Gravity and her feet propelled her forward before she realized she was moving again. For a moment, all she could hear was the blood rushing through her heart, much like the sound inside a seashell held against one's ear.

"Hey," he said.

She blinked hard then felt an involuntary smile spread across her face. "Hey."

"Here, I saved you a seat. In case you showed up." He motioned to the empty seat beside him.

"Thanks." *Wow, queen of the one word sentences much? Witty repartee like that is sure to cement our future. Snap out of it!* "It's very crowded. This must be popular."

"Oh, it's great. Totally different than the Lovecraft show, but I hope you'll like it. I'm Ethan, by the way." He reached out to shake.

She took his hand into hers and squeezed in official greeting. His hand was warm and smooth, instantly eliminating several professions: construction worker, delivery man, longshoreman. Her mind drew a blank after those. "Ethan. Yes, that fits you. Just Ethan? Like Prince?"

He laughed, and a bit of tension uncoiled from around her spine. Her shoulders relaxed, and she leaned back into her seat, settling her purse on her lap. She felt her phone vibrate inside and would bet money it was Claire.

"Ethan Lane. And you?"

"Ruby—"

The auditorium abruptly went dark except one spotlight trained upon the center of the stage. A deep, disembodied voice sounded across the theater. "Ladies and gentleman, it is my distinct pleasure to welcome you to the Annex Theatre. Please extinguish your phones now upon penalty of public humiliation should your mother call. If said faux pas should occur, we will stop, turn the spotlight upon you, and expect your immediate recitation of any of Shakespeare's lesser monologues. We will not continue until it is complete. We are reasonable people, but passionate performers. You've been warned. Let the show begin!"

So much for small talk. Ruby immediately regretted coming to a live performance for their first date. Being in the front row meant they couldn't chat at all. Rookie mistake.

Ethan leaned over and whispered in her ear, his beard tickling the side of her face. “Sorry. I just now realized the flaws in my plan of seduction. It’s been a while since I dated.”

Ruby chuckled and nodded.

Ethan reached for her hand and held it in his. He leaned back, settling in to enjoy the show, but Ruby couldn’t concentrate at all. Not with a hot stranger holding her hand in a dark theater. Hand holding was such an intimate gesture, and they’d barely spoken. But wasn’t that what she was here for? To get to know this man? What could it hurt? The Midwest part of her said to pull away, but the Seattle part of her said to enjoy the moment.

When in Seattle…

***

All Ethan could concentrate on was Ruby’s hand in his. He laughed when the audience laughed, but it was robotic because he really had no idea what was happening on the stage. All he could feel and smell was Ruby. And she smelled wonderful. Like vanilla and sunshine, the latter a precious commodity in Seattle. As he’d waited for her earlier, he’d fought the urge to bolt, leave the theater and not look back. This had all been a horrible mistake. Inviting her here. Dating. He had so much to lose. The longer he’d sat in the front row and waited, the seconds ticking by, the more his anxiety grew until finally it had been too much. He’d risen to leave when he’d spotted her…and she had spotted him. His window of opportunity closed, he’d decided to save face. Let her down easy. Complete the date but never call her again.

Seemingly against his will and certainly against his better judgment, his hand had found hers in the dark and, now, his earlier anxiety washed away with each passing moment. The time sped by. The lights glared to life, and the show was over in no time at all.

He led her out of the theater, awkwardly, toward the lobby. "What did you think?"

Ruby glanced at him and smiled shyly. "Honestly? I wasn't paying much attention."

He squeezed her hand and smiled back. "Me either. I was distracted by a beautiful brunette all night."

Ethan let go and pressed the small of her back, guiding her through the crowd to the street. They stood on the sidewalk as the crowd dissipated.

"Coffee or a drink? There's a place a couple blocks that way." He pointed in the opposite direction from her Freemont neighborhood home. "Do you know Goodfellows? We could talk there."

"No. But that sounds good. Let me text my roommate. She worries about me."

"Aw, it's good to have friends like that. No problem. My car is in the lot behind the theater. Drive or walk?"

Ruby buttoned her peacoat with one hand and texted with the other. "Let's walk," she said.

"Perfect." Ethan offered his bent arm for her to hold. She accepted, and they walked side by side toward the coffeehouse.

"Have you seen a lot of shows there?" Ruby asked.

"I try to go at least once a month. It's a good excuse to get out of the house. Otherwise, I tend to hermit in. How about you?"

"The Cthulhu show was my first."

"Lucky me, then."

"What do you do for a living?"

"Day trading. I manage a few portfolios for friends. It's actually pretty lucrative. Keeps me indoors more than I'd like. How about you?"

"I work for Google. Maps division."

"Yeah? That sounds interesting."

"It's the reason I stayed in Seattle. They offered me the job after my internship."

"You must have been very impressive. I hear they're a great company."

Goodfellows came into view, and they walked the next block in the comfortable silence of friends who'd known one another much longer than the few hours they'd spent together.

Ethan held the door open for her then followed Ruby into the busy coffeehouse. Ruby's eyes lit up as they passed the pastry display.

"Sweet tooth?" Ethan asked then smiled.

"Afraid so."

"What looks good?"

Ruby blushed. "All of it."

They picked an empty table away from the cold doorway, and Ethan helped her with her coat, laying it on the bench beside her.

"Let me get us something. Coffee?"

"Sure."

"How do you like it?"

"Black, please."

"Ah, a girl after my own heart. And a pastry, of course. Which one?"

Ruby shook her head. "You pick. I won't be able to choose."

"I think I can manage that."

Ethan shrugged out of his own jacket, retrieved his wallet and phone then went to order. The café was surprisingly busy for the late hour. The buzz of conversation echoed in the high-ceilinged room as he studied the pastry display by the front door, waiting to be served. The door opened to his right and a strong gust of icy air preceded the latest patron, a mid-thirties man with a Nikon camera dangling from a strap in front of his chest.

Ethan nodded a greeting and was thankful when the door closed again.

"What can I get for you?" the barista asked.

"Two coffees, black, and give me four of those jam thumbprint cookies, please. Two of each flavor."

The barista selected the cookies and set them onto a plate then left to retrieve their coffee. Ethan's phone rang. Irritated, he dug it out of his front jeans pocket to see who it was this late. He looked at the display. Eight missed calls. All from his agent, Ira Stone. And now he was calling again. Ira was on New York time, three hours later, which put it after 1:00 a.m. there. What the hell could be so urgent he'd call so late?

He debated whether or not to answer, but his curiosity won out. Ira wouldn't call him this late unless it was urgent.

"Ira? What's up?"

"Ethan, thank God. I've been trying to get a hold of you all night."

"Yeah, sorry about that. I was sort of on a date."

"Oh. Well. We have a problem."

The barista returned with two coffees and set them on the counter by the plate of cookies.

"Hold on, Ira."

Ethan fished out his wallet and paid with his debit card, while the barista gave him a withering glower for what he could only assume was his rudeness of being on the phone. Ethan shrugged and waited for her to run his card.

"What's going on?" Ethan asked.

"An *Inquiry* freelancer pap sent me an envelope today with more than thirty photos of you out and about in Seattle."

"That's it? Only photos?" Ethan watched steam rise from the two coffee cups.

"Yeah. Weird, right? There weren't any demands or questions. Just the photos and his business card. Ross Faraday is the guy's name. I'm worried, Ethan. I think this guy is putting things together. Or more likely has put together you're Woodring. Otherwise, why would he send photos of you…to me?"

Ethan sucked in a hard breath. "Yeah. He must not have confirmation yet, or he'd already have printed them. This is going to make things hard for me, Ira."

"I know. Seriously, though. We've had a good run. I can't believe we kept it quiet this long. Anyway, be careful. I don't know what this guy's endgame is. We're going to do some more legwork on him. I'll let you know when I know more. I wanted you to have the heads-up."

"I appreciate it. God, this is the last thing I need."

"I know. More later. Sorry to spring this on you."

"No, I'm glad you called. Talk to you soon."

"Later."

Ethan shoved his phone and wallet into his pockets and balanced the cookie plate on top of one of the cups, nearly spilling the entire production onto the cameraman behind him.

"Sorry," Ethan said, following the strap upward to the man's face. Ethan's jaw tightened as he reconsidered the Nikon around the man's neck.

"No problem."

Was he being paranoid? Slowly, as to not slosh the coffee out of the cup or topple the plate, Ethan made his way to Ruby.

"God, that took forever. Sorry," he said as Ruby took the plate and coffee cup from him and set both on the table.

"It's okay. Busy night."

"I guess so, I'm usually here earlier. Who knew it was such a hopping place in the evenings. Here." Ethan pushed the plate toward Ruby. "Lady's choice." He smiled.

Ruby chose one of the raspberry-filled cookies, and he took a lemon cookie.

Picking up his coffee mug, he motioned with it. "A toast?"

Ruby played along. "To?"

"Our dark Lord Cthulhu for bringing us together."

"May he rise again," Ruby added then took a hesitant sip, testing the temperature.

"I can't believe you saw my ad."

"I can't believe you *placed* an ad. Actually, my roommate, Claire, saw it."

"Well, thank the stars," Ethan said then took a sip of his own coffee.

Ruby took a bite of the cookie, savoring it in a decadent way that sent a shot of bad intentions straight to his groin.

It had been a long while since he'd been on a date, let alone been with a woman. His mind went blank of any possible conversation while he watched her eat. Finally, he tore his gaze away, giving himself a mental chastising for temporarily losing his focus.

"So where are you from?" Ethan asked.

Ruby leaned in and whispered like it was her deepest, darkest secret. “Nebraska.”

“Not a local, then? I can’t say I’m surprised. You seemed very…”

“What?” she demanded, crossing her arms over her chest and waiting to see what he came up with.

“Wholesome.”

“Are you saying Seattleites aren’t?” she joked.

“Not at all. You’re just different. I could tell right away. That and your affection for Lovecraft made me take the chance on the ad.”

“Ah.”

“So you sort of have a Pacific Northwest tie in. You have Oregon State’s old football coach for your Huskers now.”

Ruby snapped to attention and shook her head. “Riley? Don’t get me started.”

Ethan chuckled. “You like football, then?”

“College football. The Huskers. It’s practically a birthright. There’s not a lot to do in Nebraska. Football is life.”

“Then your life has been hard this year. What was their record?” Ethan teased.

“If you’re asking that question, you already know,” Ruby grumbled.

“Okay, so no sports talk, then. Moving on. What brought you to Seattle?”

“I’m a GIS data engineer. Like I mentioned, I work for Google Maps division. I interned there last year and got the job right out of college. I was excited to get out of the Midwest.”

“And family? Are they still all in Nebraska?”

“I have a younger brother, Kyle. He’s going to Mizzou on a football scholarship. He’s the black sheep of the family because of it.”

"What do you like to do for fun?"

"Claire and I go skiing as much as we can. Although, being a flatlander, I'm still not very good. I can finally navigate a blue slope without threat of being airlifted off the mountain."

"Well, that's something." Ethan tried the lemon cookie.

"Do you know him?" Ruby asked, nodding to someone behind him.

Ethan followed her gaze around to the cameraman who'd entered while he was ordering. He was back on the street now, outside the windows, casually pointing his camera through the glass at the barista behind the counter.

"No. Why?" Ethan asked, turning back to Ruby.

"I think he was taking pictures of us. He has been ever since you sat down."

Ethan's jaw tightened, and he could feel the heat coloring his face.

"What is it?" Ruby asked, curling her coffee-cup-warmed hand around his wrist.

"Probably nothing. Excuse me a minute, while I have a word with him." Ethan rose, pushing back the chair. Ruby held onto his wrist.

"Be careful, Ethan. Don't start anything."

"I didn't start it."

Ethan stalked out the door, locking his gaze with the man in warning. The man tightened his grip on the Nikon and hugged it close to his chest protectively as Ethan made his way toward him.

"Did you shoot photos of me and my date?" Ethan asked, his hands closing in fists at his sides.

"Yeah, I'm a photographer. It's what I do."

"Not without consent you don't. And we don't give you consent."

"The street is a public place. I can shoot anything I want. Besides why would you care as long as you're not naked or cheating on your wife. Are you cheating on your wife? Or planning to be naked soon?"

Ethan leaned in. "No. More. Photos."

"I'm not making any promises. It's a free country."

Ethan debated briefly how far to push it. As far as he knew, the guy only had photos of Ruby and the back of his head. Still. Ira's phone call was very fresh in his mind. Was this the guy? Ross Faraday?

"What's your name?" Ethan demanded.

"You tell me yours, and I'll tell you mine," the man replied.

Ethan clenched his jaw, barely containing his anger. "No more pictures."

He jabbed his finger into the man's chest for emphasis, causing the Nikon's cap to rattle against the lens. *Oops. Sorry, not sorry.* It'd be a shame if the guy's camera was damaged. What he really wanted to damage was the guy's face. Seriously.

Focusing on Ruby, he made his way back through the thickening crowd to their table. At least if the guy wanted any more shots, there would be a horde of patrons between them.

"What did he say? What did you say to him?" Ruby asked, worry crinkling her brow.

"I strongly encouraged him to stop taking our picture," Ethan said, gathering their coats. "I'm sorry to cut the night short. Do you mind if we get out of here?"

"Oh, okay. Are you famous or something? Is he paparazzi of some sort?"

"I don't know what he is, but, no, Ethan Lane is not famous." *Truth. And a lie. Great start, Lane.*

He helped Ruby into her coat then pulled on his jacket. They wove through the crowd to the door. Keeping his back to the cameraman as he went, relief flooded him as they finally entered the cold Seattle night.

Ethan reached for Ruby's hand, reassured when she offered it without hesitancy.

"I'm sorry," he said, avoiding her gaze as they walked side by side.

"It's okay. Weird, but okay."

Story of my life.

They walked back toward the theater, away from the busy coffeehouse. Ethan noticed the crowd had thinned considerably. Only one of the four street lights remained unbroken to light their way. His stomach tightened, and the hairs on the back of his neck rose at the sense they were being followed.

He smelled the man before he saw him.

Curiously, the surprise came from the alley in front of him. A man in a black ski mask and clothes stepped from the darkness and pointed a gun at them. Ethan put an arm in front of Ruby, pushing her behind him.

"Whoa, friend. No need for that. How can we help you tonight?" Ethan asked.

"Wallets. And phones. Now!" The man peered around Ethan at Ruby. "Jewelry, too."

"I…I don't have any jewelry," Ruby said.

Ethan took Ruby's phone and fished his own from his pocket. It was locked with an encrypted passcode. *Good luck breaking that, asshole.* The wallet, however, was a problem.

"Hurry. The fuck. Up!" Their assailant punctuated each word with a jerk of his gun.

Ethan opened his wallet and took out the cash, nearly three hundred dollars. He reached for Ruby's wallet before she could hand it over then emptied hers as well. He held out the cash.

The thief grabbed Ruby's wallet, and then tried to grab his, but Ethan resisted. "You have the money. Save us the hassle of new credit cards, man. You know they'll be cancelled before you can use them anyway."

The thief took a step forward and pressed the muzzle of the gun to Ethan's chest. "Wallet."

It wasn't the credit cards Ethan worried about. The only people who knew his true writing identity were his agent and publisher. He wanted to keep it that way. Not that this guy looked particularly bright…still.

Before Ethan could comply, the guy shoved Ruby hard, knocking her back into the brick wall behind them. She stumbled to the pavement. The thief grabbed Ethan's wallet from his hand and took off, running down the pitch-black alley.

"Shit. Are you okay?" Ethan asked.

Ruby nodded and put her trembling hand to the back of her head where she'd struck the wall. "Yes. I think so."

"Stay here. I'll be right back!" Ethan took chase. He needed that wallet.

"Ethan, no! He has a gun!"

Ethan kept running. He could have tracked him from scent alone. The guy reeked of stale cigarettes and meth. Chasing after the sharp chemical trail of ammonia and vinegar rolling off the man, he cursed himself as he ran. He should have picked up the warning smell earlier, but he'd been distracted by Ruby's company and the reporter. Rounding the corner, three buildings later, he caught up to him as the fat moon peeked out from behind the clouds. *Shit.* What was he doing? His adrenalin spiked as he launched himself onto the man's back. They hit the ground and skidded across the pavement. The gun slid like a hockey puck and disappeared under several large bags of trash behind a business.

The thief struggled beneath him, and Ethan grabbed at his jacket for purchase, trying to locate the wallet. He saw the flash of a blade before he felt it slice into his forearm. Black spots blinded his vision, and he knew exactly what was coming next. The shift was quick and violent. His hands elongated and his fingernails hardened and grew into claws. Hair sprouted out of every follicle, covering his body in seconds. His clothing ripped at its seams, and the man beneath him stopped struggling. For a moment, Ethan was sure he'd killed him during the shift.

"The fuck?" the thief said, scrambling away.

His awareness returning, Ethan lunged toward the man, who hesitated, his mouth open and eyes wide for only a moment, but good and long enough to take in the full measure of what he was seeing before he ran away.

Panicked, Ethan tried desperately to calm his hammering heart and slow the flood of adrenalin. The nearly full moon, high stress, and emotions on overload were the worst possible combination. No amount of shift suppressors could have prevented what had happened. He glanced over at the business's back doorway. Thank God. No cameras.

Breathe, Ethan. Breathe.

In. Out. In. Out. In. Out.

He had to shift back before Ruby came looking for him, or, worse, before there were helpful witnesses. The word of a thief would be bad enough. He certainly didn't need any fine upstanding citizens to collaborate the story of a Sasquatch in downtown Seattle.

Not now.

Not ever.

The tingle along his spine was the first indicator he was shifting back. *God, it takes forever.* Forcing it only made it worse. He pulled out every Ninja/Jedi trick he could muster to Zen himself unfurry.

This.

This was exactly why he didn't date. Why he was alone.

Why he always would be alone.

"Ethan?" Ruby said.

Oh God. Please let me be completely shifted back.

Chapter Three

Ruby kneeled beside Ethan. His clothing hung in shreds, and blood covered his right forearm.

"Ethan? Oh God, we've got to get you to the hospital."

Ethan tried to stand, but his legs buckled, refusing to cooperate. No way was he making it back to the car after shifting twice so quickly.

"My car. Can you bring my car around?" He pushed up into a sitting position.

"I don't want to leave you here, but I could run back. That man, the photographer, I think he saw it all happen. I saw him taking pictures as you ran away."

Ethan shook his head and fought like hell to tamp down his beast. *Shit! So we were being followed. And now that asshole could have photos. Of me shifting.*

"Ethan, you're bleeding. Please, let me at least go call an ambulance."

"No!" he said, more abruptly than he meant to. "No, really. I can't...I mean, I don't have health insurance. It's complicated."

"It's okay. They'll have to take you anyway. You need to see a doctor!" Ruby stood, scanning for passersby or an open business.

"I promise I'll see a doctor. I have a private physician. Please, if you could bring my car and take me home, I know I'll be fine. Really."

Ruby chewed at her lower lip. Her forehead wrinkled in a way that would have been beguiling if not for the dire situation. Protecting his secret hung on her decision.

An eternity later, she answered, "Okay. What do you drive?"

Ethan retrieved his keys from his pocket and held them out.

She stared at the keychain. "A Jaguar? You drive a Jag? I can't be responsible for that."

"It's fine. It's an old one. Not even that expensive. You'd be surprised. I trust you."

Ruby mumbled something under her breath. The only word he made out was "totaled." A spasm folded him in half, an aftereffect of the rapid shift. Painful, but it spurred Ruby into action, which was good. His chest tingled with a million pinpricks, a sign he still teetered on the brink of a shift. The last thing he wanted was to erupt into full furry in a dark alley in front of her. Or ever.

"I'll be right back. Don't move."

"Don't worry. I'm not going anywhere without you." Like he could.

She hesitated, paralyzed with indecision.

"Go," he said. "I'll be fine."

He hoped it was true.

***

Ruby hustled down the sidewalk as fast as her ridiculously high-in-light-of-current-events footwear would allow. Her mind raced with all that had occurred in such a short span of time, and her own personal soundtrack played on repeat in her brain. "Hey, I just met you and this is crazy. I'm seriously injured. Take me home, maybe?"

Shut up, brain.

Maybe she had a concussion. A head injury was the only excuse for why she now stood in a darkened parking lot in front of a black Jaguar with the keys in her hand. Was she really doing this? Not calling the cops? Not taking an injured man to the hospital? Taking her blind-date-gone-horribly-wrong…home? To *his* home?

Definitely a head injury.

Claire would kill her. If he didn't turn out to be a serial killer.

Which he probably wasn't.

God, she wished she had her phone. She briefly debated going back inside the theater to use the phone, but Ethan was bleeding on the pavement, alone. What if the thief returned before she made it back? Ethan was in amazing shape and totally looked like he could handle himself. Hell, he'd chased the guy. But the thief had a knife and a gun. She opened the door and got into the Jag.

Holy crap this is a nice car.

Okay, concentrate.

She scrambled in the dark, trying to figure out where the key went and then realized it was push-button start. The engine roared to life. Or more purred to life. It was a cat. Jaguar. Cat.

Shut up!

Her stream of consciousness was a problem on good days. This was not a good day. Not anymore.

"Go," Claire said. "It's cosmic karma," Claire said. "Maybe he's the one," Claire said.

Well, karma is a bitch and can go fuck herself.

After finally locating the lights, Ruby eased out of the parking lot, sure a giant bull's-eye flashed on her hood. "Look at me. This isn't my car. I'm about to make a horrible, potentially fatal mistake. Yes, I'm still driving."

She was only a block over, on the backside of the theater, but everything looked different from this street, in a strange car, in the dark. Was it two blocks or six back to Ethan? She caught movement to her left and spotted Ethan. He'd scooted up against the building, under the security light.

Thank God, or she might have driven by him.

He threw his hand across his face as she pulled in, squinting into the headlights. She eased up so close to him he could use the door to pull himself up and into the car.

"Sorry," she muttered. She fumbled to switch off the lights before she got out to help him, but left the engine running.

After a quick scan of the lot, she was relieved to see no sign of their assailant. He was probably draining her bank account right now. *Oh God.* He had her Google security pass, too. One of about a million phone calls she needed to make.

Ruby scurried around to the passenger side. "Let me help you."

She opened the door, and Ethan grabbed hold, pulling himself to his feet unsteadily. "Thank you," he said.

"Don't thank me yet."

He settled into the passenger seat and folded his wounded arm across his lap, holding pressure to it as best he could. Blood dripped from his elbow down the leather seat and onto the doorframe.

"This is not good, Ethan. Please let me take you to the ER. At the very least, we need to call the police."

"We will. Call the police. Just not yet. And I explained about the ER. One phone call and Jacob…Dr. Chandler will be there. He'll probably beat us home. We can call from the car, but let's get out of here first. Okay?"

Ruby searched his face, trying to ferret out his inner serial killer. Honestly, he seemed pretty harmless. He was battered and clearly exhausted. Down maybe a pint of blood from the looks of the parking lot. Thinking about it made her stomach roll with queasiness. Someone would wonder what had happened out here tomorrow.

Her nurturing instincts took over, and she shut his door, careful to not jostle his arm.

She kicked off her ridiculous shoes and carried them around to the driver's side, tossing them into the backseat. Her feet hurt. Her head hurt. And a man was bleeding in the passenger seat.

This was what she got for dating.

***

They made their way down Madison toward the Seattle Ferry Terminal. It was nearly 1:00 a.m. Ethan prayed they made the last boat across. He reached for the touchscreen to call Jacob. Talking to him in the car was dicey with Ruby along for the ride. He was positive she hadn't seen him shift, or she wouldn't have been driving him home. She was nervous enough as it was. He didn't blame her.

The phone dialed, and he spared a glance at Ruby, her knuckles white on the steering wheel, lips pursed in a thin line of concentration, as she pointedly ignored him.

Jacob answered on the third ring. "Ethan? What's wrong? It's one freakin' a.m."

"Yeah, I'm aware. Sorry. I'm on my way home…with a friend."

A long silence followed. "Friend?"

"Yeah."

"Where are you?"

"About to board the ferry. We ran into a bit of trouble. I'm gonna need some stitches and medication. You know?"

Another long pause. "And your friend?"

"She could use a look, too. Can you meet us at the house?"

"On my way. It will take me a couple of hours to motor across the bay."

"Thanks, Jacob."

Ethan ended the call.

"I'm fine," Ruby said.

"I know. But it doesn't hurt to check." Ethan sent her a halfhearted smile.

Ruby exited Madison and wound her way through the quiet back streets. Traffic was light. All reasonable people were in bed.

Ethan readjusted in his seat. "Maybe I can drive. You could call a cab from the dock." He tried to raise his injured arm to show her he could, and his vision went black.

"Yeah. That's totally going to work," she said, pulling into the ferry lot. They followed the signs to the ticketing kiosk. "Problem. We have no money."

"Tip down the visor. I have a commuter pass."

Ruby retrieved the pass, but not before she got a glimpse of herself in the mirror. She grimaced.

"You should have seen the other guy," Ethan joked.

"I did. Very clearly. It will all be in my police report."

Ethan swallowed hard. She was a dog with a bone. No way she'd let this go. He really needed her to let it go.

Ruby inserted the pass into the kiosk and the arm rose, allowing them to pass through. An attendant waved them forward. They drove up onto the ferry and parked. She tipped her head back against the headrest and sighed. Ethan watched the attendant close the gate, and the ferry shuddered to life. They pulled away from the dock moments later.

Maybe their luck was changing.

"I should call Claire now. She's probably already called the police and reported me missing. She'll want to come and get me."

Ethan closed his eyes. So much for their good luck.

"I'm sorry. This is the last ferry until 6:10 a.m. I'm afraid it's a one-way trip."

Chapter Four

Un. Freakin'. Believable.

And this is what being a Good Samaritan got you. Stuck in a car, headed to an island with a more-than-likely-not-a-serial-killing stranger. A hot stranger. Still. Ruby's internal alarm bells were at DEFCON 1. This was so not a good idea.

Claire told her all the time she was too trusting. She blamed growing up in the Midwest. Folks looked out for one another, helped out their kids, families, neighbors whenever and wherever they were needed. Sure, there were some bad apples, but most of the time folks left their houses and cars unlocked, and kids walked home from school and rode their bikes through town.

Seattle had been an eye-opener: liberal, diverse, and crowded, but also fun, exciting, and freeing. Her parents had only flown up once since she'd started at Google last summer, soon after graduation. She couldn't decide who would be more shocked by her driving Ethan home, her parents or Claire. She was slightly more afraid of Claire.

She wanted to talk to her, but she also wanted some privacy to do it. She wasn't mad at Ethan.

Angrier with herself for not realizing the situation she put herself into. So far, at least, Ethan had been a perfect gentleman. Right up to the point where it had all gone to hell.

"You can still call," Ethan offered.

"I'll wait until we get to your house. She's going to freak. It won't be pretty."

"I'll make sure you get home safely. First thing in the morning." He checked the dash clock. "Maybe brunch. Morning is getting shorter and shorter. I have a nice guest room." Ethan stared out his window. "This wasn't the way I had hoped our night would end."

"What? You didn't plan all along to get sliced open by a mugger then take me home?"

God bless him, he actually blushed. The tops of his cheeks colored, and he smiled at her, suddenly becoming the most adorable man in the universe again. A shiver that had nothing to do with the temperature ran down her spine. She liked him. Besides, things had to get better from here. Right?

He leaned in, and she didn't hesitate. His warm lips touched hers, and the past couple of hours of anxiety melted away. His tongue parted her lips, and she kissed him back. His beard and mustache tickled her nose, but she liked it. She'd never kissed a man with this much facial hair before. She slid her hand up and behind his head, into his hair. Probably the thickest she'd ever seen on a man, soft and silky. He twisted in his seat, moving his arm to embrace her then sucked in a hard breath instead.

"Are you okay?" she asked.

"Yeah, forgot about my arm there for a moment."

"Sorry."

"I'm not. That kiss was totally worth it."

It was her turn to blush. It was a good kiss.

The ferry slowed, the moment broken. Bainbridge dock came into view.

Ruby followed Ethan's directions and pulled into his driveway an hour later. Bainbridge was a big island, but this house seemed to cover half of it. Massive. A masterpiece of Arts and Crafts style architecture, it loomed into the night sky as she drove into his wood-paneled, four-car garage. Day trading must be much more lucrative than working at Google as a mapping monkey. The doors lowered behind them, and she turned off the engine.

"Home sweet home." Ethan fumbled with the handle, trying to get out.

"Let me help you," Ruby said, exiting the car.

She hurried around to his side and opened it for him. Ethan unfolded himself from the cramped interior and towered over her, causing her heart to accelerate again.

"Jacob will be here soon. Let's get inside." Ethan led the way up two steps and into the house.

Ruby gasped when lights automatically illuminated an amazing, lofted living area. Seattle's skyline, across the Sound, twinkled through floor-to-ceiling windows. She'd never seen the city look more beautiful. Forgetting her host, she found herself standing directly against the window, taking it all in. Something about his story didn't add up. *He drives a luxury car, lives in an extravagantly expensive home, and doesn't have health insurance?*

She felt Ethan encroach into her space. "That view is why I bought this house. I looked at dozens along the coast but this one…was the best." A drop of blood splashed on the hardwood floor behind her and she whipped around, startled back to reality.

"You need to put pressure on that wound," Ruby said, putting a bit of distance between them.

"You're right. Please excuse me. Phone is there." He pointed to a massive desk in front of a mammoth wall library. "I'll be right back. Call your friend."

Ruby nodded and watched him walk away, disappearing down a long hallway. Resisting the urge to peruse his bookshelf, she got down to the business at hand. The phone was an old rotary style number, not a retro reproduction but a heavy-as-hell, metal-based light-blue phone. God, her grandma still had one of these babies. Using her index finger, she cranked the dial around, one number at a time, until it began to ring through.

"Where. The. Hell. Are. You?" Claire asked, on the third ring.

"I'm fine. It's a long, long story which still isn't over. I'm on Bainbridge."

"The island? What the fuck are you doing on the island? You were a mile from our house! Ruby, where are you? Exactly. I'm coming to get you."

Ruby twisted the phone cord around her hand. "You can't. The next ferry isn't until 6:00 a.m. I'm at Ethan's house. We had a little problem. We got mugged."

Ruby pulled the phone away from her ear as Claire launched into a barrage of curses on her behalf. She could still hear her clearly, just slightly less emphatically. When the torrent slowed, she cut in.

"I'm fine, Claire. It was scary, but we're okay. Mostly. Ethan was cut. He refused to go to the hospital or let me call the police but his doctor friend is on the way."

"There are about twelve red flags in those last two comments, Ruby. Have you lost your sense of self-preservation completely? Screw Ethan. I already went to the police. I drove by the theater at midnight and you were nowhere to be found. I got a little crazy. I'm getting back from the station now. I wanted them to put out an Amber Alert or something on you but they refused. Said you weren't officially missing until—Oh. My. God."

"What? What is it, Claire?" Ruby took a step toward the glass windows, toward Seattle and her friend. "Claire?"

"Our door has been kicked open," Claire said.

"Don't go in there! The thief took our wallets. He'll have our addresses. Turn around and go back to the police station."

"No way! No one breaks into my house!"

"Claire! Claire!" Ruby panicked, her heart thundering in her chest. Why, oh why didn't her friend practice what she preached and use some precautions of her own? The helplessness of her situation nearly overwhelmed her. All she could do was call her name and wait. Maybe that's what Claire felt all the time, protecting her naive Midwestern friend. Ruby sat down hard in the leather office chair and pressed her trembling hand to her forehead. The burst of adrenalin made her nauseous as she listened to the open line. Nothing but steps and static.

"You still there?" Claire asked.

"Yes! What's happening? You're giving me a heart attack."

"Welcome to the club. No one's here. The house has been trashed, though. Someone was most definitely here. All of our electronics are gone. At least the portable ones: iPads, laptops. So that sucks."

“At least you weren’t home when he was there. What a mess! Still think answering that ad was a good idea?”

A long silence filled the space between them. “I’m sorry, Ruby. I got you into this mess. I promise I’ll get you out. Somehow. Where’s Ethan now?”

Ruby looked toward the hallway, where he had disappeared nearly fifteen minutes ago. “He went to care for his wound. He’s been gone a while. I should probably go check on him.”

“Do you feel safe with him there?”

“Yes.”

“There’s a police substation on Bainbridge. If anything happens…anything…you leave that house and get there. I’ll take care of things on this end. I’ll be on the first ferry this morning to get you. What’s your address? And what’s Ethan’s last name?”

“His last name is Lane. I don’t know the address. He directed me here.”

“Look around for some mail,” Claire said.

“Right.” Ruby sorted through the papers on his desk. Several envelopes addressed to Robin Woodring but none to Ethan Lane. “I’m not seeing anything with Ethan’s name on it here. Just some to a Robin Woodring, and it’s addressed to a NY post office box.”

“Robin Woodring?” Claire asked, followed by a long pause. “The horror author?”

A spark of recognition ignited in Ruby. She spun around in the chair and faced the library wall behind her. One entire section was devoted to writing craft, the other three were horror novels, and the center section was entirely compromised of Robin Woodring books. Hardbacks. First editions from the looks of them.

What the hell was going on here?

She spotted another pile of mail on the kitchen counter, but couldn't make it over to it with the corded phone. "Hold on a minute."

Ruby headed into the kitchen, sparing a glance down the hallway where Ethan had gone. No sign of him. She sorted through the pile of retail flyers and bills, all addressed to Ethan Lane at 2033 Cove Sound Road.

Ethan Lane? Robin Woodring?

Holy shit! Ethan is Robin. Robin is Ethan.

No wonder he didn't want to go to the police or the hospital. Robin Woodring was renowned as one of the most reclusive writers ever. He was the Harper Lee of horror. Reporters and critics had been trying to crack his pen name for years. Years! She'd read his books in high school: *The Shimmering, Grave Teller, Goodwin Hollow*. A shiver ran down her spine remembering them. How could he be so young? She'd imagined him much older. More…unEthanlike.

The phone receiver vibrated across the desk with Claire's pleas. Ruby gathered her senses and carried the counter mail back to the desk.

"You aren't going to believe this," Ruby said. "Ethan is Robin Woodring."

Dead silence.

"Claire?"

"Yeah. Processing."

More silence.

"You went on a date and got mugged with Robin Woodring. *The* Robin Woodring."

"All indications appear so."

"This night keeps getting weirder. Guess that would make more sense out of why he was hospital and cop shy."

"That's what I'm thinking. Listen, we can't tell anyone. He's a nice guy. And…he's freakin' Robin Woodring! Seriously, don't tell anyone, Claire. Please."

Claire snorted. "As long as you get home safe and sound first thing in the morning, his secret is safe with me. But if he lays a hand on you, I'll rain down Hell on him. You tell him *that*."

Ruby smiled. "Will do. Do you feel safe there? After the break-in?"

"I'm fine. I'll hang out until the police make it over. I suppose you two are safe until morning, considering the only way the mugger is getting onto the island is if he steals a boat. I'm doubting he'll be that motivated. God, this is all kinds of messed up. What's the address?"

"Oh, I almost forgot! Twenty thirty-three Cove Sound Road. I'd better go check on Ethan. He's been gone a long time. You have the address and phone number now. I'll see you in the morning…erm…later."

"Good night, Ruby. Be careful."

"I will. Thanks, Claire. I love you hard."

"Ditto."

Chapter Five

Ross Faraday's hands trembled as he pressed the SD card into his computer. This wasn't the first crime he'd witnessed and captured with his camera, but the images flashing across his screen in tiny thumbnails as they imported, already had his heart racing. He'd seen the event unfold with his own eyes then followed Lane into the alley, hoping to capture something juicy enough to use against Lane as he confronted his assailant.

He was 99 percent sure Ethan Lane was in fact Robin Woodring. This would be the story of his career if he could break it. The last photo on his screen both thrilled and terrified him. This wasn't a grainy or blurred image. This was the most impressive, high definition still photo of a Bigfoot he'd ever seen. There was no mistaking it for a man in a monkey suit. You couldn't fake that musculature, the glow of those red eyes, or the expression of pure rage on the creature's face. A creature, who six shots earlier, had been Ethan Lane.

He had him. The entire progression from man to beast to man again. Hell, it didn't even matter anymore if the guy was Robin Woodring. This was monumental.

Faraday pushed his rolling chair back from his desk and stroked his hand thoughtfully across his growing chin stubble. He reached for the bottle of acid controller standing sentry by his computer. His ulcer was on fire. Possibilities flashed through his mind. Who to call first?

He'd followed the mugger for a few blocks after Ethan had shifted back but lost him and abandoned the chase. Faraday already knew where Ethan lived. He'd been through his mail and garbage countless times when the man had left for trips into the city, but still had nothing linking him to Woodring other than the agent's name posted on Woodring's fan site as his contact. A fact anyone with the Internet who was interested knew as well. He'd actually stalked the agent more than Ethan, and when he'd followed the agent to a New York City post office box to retrieve mail, things began to click into place for him.

Why not send an assistant for such a menial task? Unless you couldn't trust anyone else to do the job. Faraday was betting his career the agent was picking up fan mail for Woodring, yet he had no proof other than his hunches. But now? With this latest development? None of that seemed relevant. The horror writer's true identity would be trumped by his true nature.

Dare he confront the man? Ask for an interview? After their encounter in the coffeehouse, he doubted his request would be well tolerated. But, now, he had much more leverage. Not proof of his Woodring connection, but proof of so much more.

The *Inquiry* would pay dearly for the shots, but the underlying story would be worth so much more.

He emailed the photos to his phone then googled the *Bigfoot Hunting Department* reality television show's lead hunter, Garret Decker. He needed an ally. If he was lucky, he could blow both stories wide open.

He'd be a legend.

And very, very rich.

***

Ruby walked through the silent house and down the long hallway, peeking through numerous doorways. The house was huge and a maze. One entire room was devoted to classic horror movie memorabilia, another to Sasquatch. Talk about the boy who never grew up!

She followed the trail of blood droplets along the hardwood floors to a set of double doors. The lights turned on as soon as she entered. The master suite was bathed in rich chocolate brown and cream. Huge pine beams tented across the ceiling above a king-sized bed.

"Ethan?" The blood drops disappeared through the master bath doorway. "Ethan?" she repeated. She didn't want to invade his privacy, but, when he didn't answer, she forged ahead.

"Oh, no!" He lay in a rapidly growing pool of blood. Moonlight shone through the round bathroom window, but the lights didn't come on in here like they had in the master suite.

He'd removed his tattered shirt before passing out on the cold stone floor. He lay facedown, his head resting on his unwounded arm, which had likely saved him from a head injury. His back was to the door.

Ruby hurried to his side. He'd managed to bandage his wounded arm, but blood soaked the gauze wrap.

Where is that doctor?

She knew now why he hadn't wanted to call for help, but was his secret worth dying for? Of course not! She felt along his neck for a pulse and was relieved to find a steady if not overly strong thrum there. She pulled a fluffy towel from the rack behind her and placed it behind his head before rolling him over. As she turned him onto his back, she gasped.

His face! His chest!

His beard had grown since they'd arrived home. It was a good six inches longer than when they'd left the theater. And his chest was a carpet of thick reddish-brown hair as well. She began to inspect him more closely. His back was a smooth and hairless mass of muscle. She'd always had a thing for hairy men, but geez Louise! He was giving the Wolfman a run for his money. It was just like in his book, *Rise of the Sasquatch!* And his muscles? Maybe it was his lack of a shirt, but he hadn't seemed nearly as bulky and defined fully dressed. It made her wonder what was going on under the rest of his clothes. Her eyes settled on his groin briefly before she forced herself to return to the problem at hand. *Bleeding. Definitely need to staunch the bleeding.*

She pressed her palm to his wound and held the pressure there as she sat beside him on the floor. She didn't know what else to do for him. He'd made it abundantly clear he didn't want any authorities called, and she'd heard his friend Jacob say he was on his way. All she could do was sit with him and wait. A million thoughts raced through her mind as she tried to piece together the night. It was like she'd fallen into another dimension. She was so far out of her element.

She couldn't have imagined a stranger night. She reached for another towel and wiped up the cold, sticky blood as best she could. It was a mess.

"Ethan?" she said, her voice sounded weak and unsure even to herself. "Ethan, please wake up."

He didn't. She stroked her palm across his roughened cheek and bent to kiss his forehead. He was hot to the touch. Too hot. Panic rose in her again. Screw it. She was calling an ambulance. He'd just have to deal with it. Removing her hand from the wound, she waited for a moment to see if the bleeding had lessened. When it seemed to have stopped, she walked into the bedroom to look for a phone. She searched the room, amazed he wouldn't have a phone in the master. She raced out into the hallway toward the desk phone and ran headlong into a man.

"Shit!" She struggled to free herself from his solid grip as he held her steady.

"You must be 'the friend'?" he asked.

"Since you're not the thief, you must be the doctor? And you have a key?" she asked, surprised.

"I'm also his friend. So, yes. I have a key. Jacob Chandler. Where's Ethan?"

"He's back here." Ruby led Jacob to the bathroom. "So, if you're a friend with a key, I guess you know why he wouldn't let me take him to the ER or call the police. I mean, I guess you know his secret?"

Jacob grabbed hold of her upper arm and spun her around to face him.

Ruby gulped. Jacob wasn't quite as tall as Ethan, but he was somehow more intimidating. A five o'clock shadow covered his sharp jaw, and his dark-brown eyes bore down on her. "What secret would that be?" he asked.

"Nothing. I…I thought there must be…" Ruby swallowed hard before proceeding. "A really good reason."

Gah! No need to dig herself in further. *Stop talking already!*

Ruby broke eye contact and stared down at the floor.

"Is that his blood?" he asked.

"Yes, there's a whole lot more in the bathroom."

Ruby walked into the master bath first and came to a dead stop. Her mouth gaped open as her brain struggled to process what she was seeing. Jacob followed quickly then pushed her aside. Her hip knocked against the bath vanity, the pain giving her something else to focus on as her brain caught up.

A monster lay on the bathroom floor where she'd left Ethan moments ago, a beast covered in long, reddish-brown hair from head to gigantic foot. His previously handsome face had morphed and swollen. His forehead protruded in a cruel, prehistoric ridge. His mouth parted slightly as a rapid, huffing pant emanated, revealing animalistic teeth. Shredded clothing lay on either side of the creature. Its bulk was squeezed between the long bath vanity and the walk-in shower. Even though she saw it, she couldn't form any words. In her heart, she knew it was Ethan there on the floor, but her mind couldn't reckon it.

She blinked hard and slow, shaking her head a little, trying to make sense of it all.

"Ethan?" Jacob shook his shoulders hard then pried the creature's eyes open with his thumb and finger. He pulled a small pen light from his jacket pocket and shone the beam into the beast's eye. Red filled its iris where Ethan's had been blue earlier. He repeated the act on his other eye then checked for a pulse, seemingly unaware and unmoved by his friend's current state.

What. The. Hell?

Ruby's brain reengaged and a scream gathered from deep within her, threatening to unleash in the tiny room. She began to hyperventilate.

Jacob pulled a syringe from his other pocket, uncapped it, and injected the monster—Ethan—in the neck. Ruby bent over the sink, struggling not to vomit. The stress, the adrenalin, all of it flooded through her. Jacob laid his ear to the creature's chest and listened.

Ruby started to back out of the doorway.

"Stay right here. You need to see this," Jacob commanded, without looking at her.

She froze, half in, half out of the bathroom, but as far away from both of them as possible.

The moonlight lessened, and the room darkened briefly before the automatic lights clicked on, flooding the room with bright light. There was no mistaking what lay on the floor before her now.

Sasquatch, her brain said.

Seconds later, the monster began to convulse and writhe on the floor. Jacob pressed his hands against the monster's shoulders holding it firmly against the floor, trying to prevent it from thrashing into the cabinet or marble shower. The visible fur began to stiffen and stand on end then slowly shortened as it retracted and absorbed into the beast's body, leaving a nearly hairless and completely naked Ethan Lane in its place.

Ruby's legs crumpled beneath her, and she sank to the floor. The doorframe the only thing keeping her upright. Her body felt like a human gummy worm.

Ethan's eyes fluttered open. He stared at them both for several long seconds, before recognition shown on his face.

"Jacob?" he asked.

"Yeah, buddy. I'm here. And so is…" Jacob leaned back so Ethan would have a full view of the doorway. "Your 'friend.'"

"Oh God," Ethan said. "Jacob, I'm sorry. I…I…I wanted to go on a date. You know?"

"Yeah. I know."

"I shifted?"

"Oh yeah."

"Shit."

Ruby felt like she was floating above the scene in some sort of out-of-body experience because there was no freakin' way she was awake and aware on an island in a horror writer/Sasquatch's bathroom.

Nope.

Clearly, she'd endured a head injury. This was all a dream. A nice drug or coma-induced dream. She'd have a good laugh over all of this with Claire just as soon as she woke up. And then she'd never, ever, ever date again. Hell, she might give up reading after this. She'd read too many books, and now they were all jumbled up in her head in some sort of mental stew of stories that was leaking out in her dreams.

Yep, that was it.

"Ruby?" Ethan said. "Ruby." Ethan sat up quickly, and Jacob caught his shoulders before he slammed his head into the cabinet.

"Easy there, E. You've shifted at least a couple of times way too rapidly. That's probably why you passed out earlier. Give it a minute. I shot you up with suppressant. You're going to have a hell of a headache, but you shouldn't have to worry about shifting accidentally again for a while. We need to get you to the reservation so you can get it out of your system. How long since you shifted on purpose?"

Ethan looked at Ruby then back to Jacob.

"She's already seen everything you have to offer man. In for a penny, in for a pound. It's not like we can take it all back now," Jacob said.

"Joseph's going to stroke," Ethan said.

"Probably." Jacob sighed. "How long, Ethan?"

"Six months or so."

"Six months? No wonder you blew up. You know better than this."

"I want a normal life, Jacob."

"Well, that ship sailed a long time ago. Let's get you both to the boat and back to the reservation."

Ruby snapped to attention. "What? No way. Claire is coming to pick me up. I'm not going anywhere until she gets here."

Jacob turned toward her, rising to his full height over her. "Lady, you're going with us until we're sure you're not a threat to Ethan or the rest of us."

"The rest of us?" Ruby asked.

Jacob's eyes flashed red for a split second. "The rest of us."

"Oh!" Ruby recoiled in fear, taking a long, quick step back.

"Jacob! Stop scaring her. She saved my life. Hell, she probably saved all of us. She could have left me in that alley or taken me to a hospital. I think you know exactly how that would have ended," Ethan said, rising to his feet as he pulled himself up with the countertop. "Do you want the entire clan exposed?"

Jacob fumed, his hands curling and uncurling at his sides. "No."

"Then, ease up. It's a lot to take in. Go get the boat ready. We'll be out in a few minutes. I need to pack a few things first…and talk to Ruby."

Jacob stood, unmoving, longer than was comfortable then stormed past her and out of sight.

Ruby let out the breath she'd been holding. Ethan grabbed another clean towel from the shelf over the toilet and wrapped it around his waist, but not before Ruby got a good long look at…everything.

Holy shit!

Her face heated, and she turned away, hoping he hadn't noticed her gawking.

She'd watched her date change from a man to a monster to a man, and she was still checking out his package? What was wrong with her?

Of course, now that he was Ethan again, it all seemed sort of ridiculous. Coma dreams were like that.

"So now you know my secret." Ethan closed the distance between them.

Ruby looked down at his arm. A thin, white scar was the only trace of his encounter with the mugger. His arm had healed completely. She reached to touch it, and her fingertips brushed against a fine fluff of tiny soft hairs sprouting there.

"You're healed? Already?"

"It's the shifting. The change can heal most injuries, except the basic mortal ones that could have killed me as a human."

"You're not human, then?"

"I'm 99 percent human. Think human with benefits."

"And I thought I'd already discovered your big secret," she said.

"Oh, so you figured that out, too, did you?"

“Yes…you’re…” She hesitated.

“Yes, it’s true. I’m sorry. I didn’t want you to know. No one knows.”

“You’re a…a…” she stammered.

“A horror writer? Yes.” Ethan bent his head and grasped her chin gently, lifting her face to his. She stared up into his blue, blue eyes. “And a Sasquatch.”

Chapter Six

Ethan walked into the upper cabin of the cruiser, where Jacob sat at the helm. The boat skipped across the smooth water in the early morning before the Sound got busy with tourists and traffic. The sunrise began to tint the horizon in pinks and purples as they headed to the Lummi Reservation. He'd left Ruby in the hold below, sitting on the couch and talking to her friend on the boat's satellite phone. It took everything he had in him not to stand at the door and listen in on what she was telling the girl. Ruby wasn't a prisoner.

He'd made that as clear as he could, but he couldn't exactly let her run home before he had a chance to convince her, to his satisfaction, keeping their secret was in her best interests. If the clan found out, or if she spoke to the media, he didn't want to think about what would happen. He already knew. The clan would ruin her reputation, her career, and her life, or worse, if she started spouting off nonsense about seeing a Sasquatch shifter. Not to mention what it would do to his writing career when they discovered that little transgression.

Of course, Jacob knew about the writing. Had for years. Jacob, Ethan's agent, and the CEO of his publisher were the only ones on the planet who knew. Until now. At this point, he wasn't sure which secret was in the most jeopardy. He hadn't had a chance to tell Jacob about the most recent development with the photographer who he was now certain he'd met face-to-face in the coffeehouse a few hours ago. *Ross Faraday. Jesus.*

Either way, as far as the clan was concerned, he was screwed. No one. Ever. In the history of Sasquatches had allowed a civilian to watch them shift and gone unpunished. Thank God, the clan didn't know yet and, hopefully, they never would. Ruby would be safe with him on the reservation as a guest until things blew over and Jacob made sure the thief was contained. The photographer was an entirely different problem. Depending on how much he saw and what sort of photos he had in his possession, he'd have to be dealt with.

While he didn't want Ruby any more involved than she already was, he did want to keep her safe. He owed her that much. It was his own fault. All of it. He should never have tried to live among the normals. To *be* normal. His hubris had ruined everything.

"How's our passenger?" Jacob asked.

"Talking to her friend."

"You think that's a good idea?"

"From what Ruby told me, the girl seemed pretty hell-bent on coming for her. She had my address, my name—both of my names. I didn't see an option. I trust Ruby to be discreet."

Jacob laughed then sighed. "Yeah, we're all kinds of discreet." He handed Ethan his cell phone. "Click play."

Ethan took the phone and hit the arrow. A *King5 Breaking News* report began to play. Ethan watched the grainy video of him in his Sasquatch form throwing off his attacker. Nothing was clear, thank God. With no lights near the business, it was hard to tell what was happening. But one of the two human forms could easily have been mistaken for a man in a gorilla suit…or a Sasquatch. Later, his car pulled into the lot, its lights blinding the camera and rendering the rest of the recording unusable. It was all dark, him, his car, everything, but it was clear enough something was going on. And Pacific Northwest imaginations were fertile.

Ethan clenched his jaw. “Jesus.”

“But wait, there’s more.” Jacob snatched back the phone and opened his email then showed it to Ethan.

Council Tribunal Elders to convene this evening at 6:00 p.m. to discuss recent activity in downtown Seattle. Cleaner crew will be dispatched. Any known activity must be reported immediately.

“So they already know?” Ethan asked, shocked.

“Welcome to the twenty-first century, my friend. Your thief called the station and gave an interview, failing to mention the assault he perpetrated on you and your lady friend. He’s not really sure what happened. Thinks maybe it was…wait for it…a Sasquatch. Said he found a wallet in the same area. He’s not the most credible witness, but you can bet someone official probably has your wallet by now. He seems to be making things up as he goes. So, yeah, I’d say they know. Our guy in the Seattle PD will be all over this. How do you want to play it? With the clan?” Jacob asked.

Ethan shook his head in disbelief. “Goddamn it. Obviously, I want to minimize the impact on Ruby. It would also be really great if my pen name wasn't blown to hell. I hold out the most minimal of hope for either of those things. I may have another problem."

"What's that?"

"A photographer named Ross Faraday sent photos of me to my agent. I think he was in the coffeehouse tonight, taking photos of me with Ruby. He's trying to out me as Woodring but hasn't made the connection for certain yet. He may have followed us and taken more photos."

"Of you shifting?" Jacob asked, incredulous.

"I don't know. God, I hope not."

A long silence stretched between them.

"You need to shift. A good, long shifted run will do more for your frame of mind than anything else. Don't wait, Ethan. Get it out of your system. We'll deal with this. One problem at a time."

"Yeah," Ethan said, not believing his friend's comforting words for a minute. This was beyond anything he could ever have plotted for one of his books.

"Your thief," Jacob said. "He's gonna want proof to collaborate his story. They always do. A footprint. Hair. A dead Sasquatch. Not to mention the Bigfoot hunters this is going to activate. Yeah, you got ninety-nine problems, my friend."

Ethan ran a hand through his hair. "Ruby said the thief had already been to her house. He trashed the place and stole their electronics. Shit. He's probably already headed to my place."

"Not yet. It'd be way too brazen to break in during broad daylight. Besides, the ferry's just started running. Unless he chartered a boat or took his own to the island, he'll wait. I'd expect him tonight, though. You're gonna have your hands full with Ruby and the clan council. I'll take a cleaner team and look for him. I'll go to Ruby's roommate and feel her out, see what she knows."

"Okay. I told Ruby you can pick up some clothes for her. That's as good a reason as any to visit the roommate."

"Exactly. Then we'll set up shop and wait for him at your place. He won't want to mug anyone or tell any Sasquatch stories after we're done with him."

"You can't kill them, Jacob. Either of them."

Jacob shot Ethan a hard look. "How many times have I done this, Ethan? More than likely, we'll put the whammy on him, after we have a little fun. I'm not going to kill anyone. It hardly ever comes to that."

Ethan shuddered. The whammy was almost as good as dead.

"Make sure it doesn't. Please. I can't have their deaths on my conscience on top of everything else."

"Think of it as fodder for your next book. Just change the Sasquatches to vampires. It will be another bestseller."

"Smartass."

"It's how I roll."

"God, what a mess."

"That it is." Jacob banked a hard right around Lummi Island, pitching Ethan into the cabin wall. He saw Ruby below, through the window, still talking to her friend.

"If you hadn't shown up when you did…if Ruby had left me there to be found, or if I had hurt her…"

"None of that happened. There's a way out of this. We'll make it right."

Ethan snorted. "I'm glad one of us thinks so."

"Go down there and start working your magic on her."

“And what magic would that be?”

Jacob smiled. “Whatever magic you can conjure. Better you than the clan.”

Ethan’s stomach sank. He didn’t want anything bad happening to Ruby because of him. Knowing him had already put her in danger. He liked her. Even now. Especially now. The thought of the clan ruining her promising career at best, or her mind and personality at worst, was untenable. But Jacob was right. If he didn’t thoroughly convince the council she wouldn’t be a problem, all would be lost. For them both.

***

“I don’t like this,” Claire said. Ruby could practically feel her pacing the room on the other end of the line.

“I know. He’s worried about the thief. I’m not being kidnapped.” Well, not exactly.

“I don’t understand why you—we—don’t just let the police handle this. The asshole’s already been here. Why would he come back? What would he possibly have to gain by doing that? He already took everything. It would be stupid to come back. I mean, I can understand Ethan not wanting his cover blown and all but…really? Really?”

Ruby understood her frustration. She hadn’t said a word about the other problem, the Sasquatch problem, which was the real reason behind the charade and why she was on a boat to some Indian reservation. She’d seen too much. The last thing she wanted was to drag Claire into it deeper. No, she’d have to handle this herself. She *would* handle this herself. Claire already knew too much about Ethan’s writing and his pen name, but she was pretty sure *that* wouldn't get her friend killed. This other secret? Even after watching Ethan shift into that…monster, now that he was the same sweet and funny guy she'd met at the theater, it was harder to believe any of it had ever happened. Secretly, she was hanging onto the coma-dream theory, but it was getting less plausible by the minute. But if it wasn't a dream, she'd stumbled into a world of shit she was completely unprepared for.

In her heart, she knew what she'd seen was real. Ethan was a monster. No matter how kind and amazingly cute he looked now, his true self had been revealed on that bathroom floor. This wasn't the sort of thing a girl could escape from. It was time to stop dreaming and face things head on. So why wasn't she trying harder to run away? Because this Ethan, the one who wasn't a monster, was also real, and she needed to somehow reconcile the two of them.

"I know it all sounds crazy. Listen, Ethan's friend, Jacob, is coming to pick up some things for me. Would you mind packing some clothes? You know what I need. Send enough for a week."

"A week? Ruby, you'll lose your job if you're gone a week!"

"I'm going to call in sick. You'll have to cover for me."

"They'll want a doctor's note to verify that. How are you going to work that miracle?"

"Jacob is a doctor."

"Well, of course he is. Jesus Christ. I wish I knew what was going on. You aren't telling me everything. You're probably trying to protect me. Stop it. I can't help you unless I know what's really going on. All of it."

Ruby hesitated too long in replying.

"Your silence is consent, you know."

"It's not. I appreciate you, Claire. Don't worry about me. I'm fine. I'll be fine. Next week, we'll laugh about all of this."

"I don't feel like laughing."

Ethan paused at the top of the stairs, warning her of his arrival. "I have to go. I'll call you when I can. Take care of things at home and don't give Jacob a hard time when he comes to get my stuff."

"No promises there. Be careful, Ruby. I love you."

Ruby swallowed the lump in her throat and closed her burning eyes. "I love you, too, Claire. Bye."

Ethan made his way down the stairs, and she swiped at her teary eyes. Crying was such a girl thing to do. It pissed her off. She needed to be strong on the outside, even if her insides were in turmoil.

"Everything okay?" Ethan asked, fumbling nervously with his hands.

"Yeah. She's pretty pissed and unhappy about the whole thing, but at least she's not gathering an army…yet."

"Well, that's a plus." Ethan sat on the leather bench opposite her. The cabin was beautiful. High-gloss red teakwood and leather upholstery. The long benches curved around the prow on one end, and a bar lined the opposite wall under the stairs. Neon bar signs glowed, advertising Pike's Place Porter and Bainbridge Brews. A full kitchen took up the space in between. More steps led down to a lower level Ruby hadn't had the guts to explore.

The boat lurched over a wave, and her stomach did a little flip-flop as she grabbed a brass handrail along the wall behind her.

"I think a storm is blowing in, but don't worry, we're almost there," Ethan said.

Ruby nodded and looked out the large cabin window behind her at the sea.

"Where are we going, Ethan? I mean, you told me where, the Lummi Reservation, but why there? What is it, really?"

Ethan bent forward with his forearms resting on his thighs. He threaded his fingers together as if in prayer, working his thumbs over one another repeatedly.

"The Lummi have protected our kind for as long as we've both existed. In pre-colonial times, the tribe migrated through the many islands all over the Pacific Northwest. Those days were easy and both the Lummi and the Sasquatch clans flourished. Both of our peoples were fishermen, and hunter gatherers. The land was wild and free, and so were we. But then the Lummi were confined to a reservation, and it became harder and harder for both of us to live."

"And the Lummi knew—know—what you are?"

Ethan blushed. Even beneath his growing beard, she could see him color. His face had been clean-shaven when they'd left his home two hours ago.

"The adults do. It's a rite of passage to be shown the secrets of the Sasquatch and become a keeper of the past. The Lummi call us *Ts'emekwes*. Other tribes have different names and stories, but the bond between Sasquatch and indigenous people is strong. We are human but also more. Shifters. The Lummi think our ability is a gift from the Great Spirit and our abilities a remnant of the Creator's desire to experience the world he's made. The moon drives us. We shift and run the woods of the reservation or the wilds of the deep woods until the urge passes. The rest of the time, we're fishermen and bankers and plumbers and…writers." Ethan smiled at her.

Ruby curled up tighter on the couch, drawing her legs beneath her.

"The moon wasn't full last night. Not yet. So why did you…shift?"

"Jacob is our clan doctor. For obvious reasons, we can't go to the hospital. Our DNA is insane. Part ape/part humanoid/and part extinct Neanderthal. Through the years, the shamans and our own doctors have developed a vaccine to suppress the shift. But it's only a temporary solution for those who refuse to live on the reservation. If one suppresses the change too long, it's bound to happen when we can't control it. I think the stress of the attack triggered me, and once it was unleashed…"

"So you're a Neanderthal? And you've always been this way?"

"Part Neanderthal, thanks. And yes. It's an inherited trait. Offspring born to two full Squatch parents are 100 percent guaranteed to carry the trait as well."

"And those from mixed parentage?" Ruby asked.

"Mating monogamously with a human breaks the cycle of shifting eventually. Sometimes, it can take up to a year. Their offspring will not carry the trait."

Ruby twisted her ring around her finger. "Does that happen a lot? Mating with humans?"

Ethan sighed. "The clan council forbids it. Our race is dwindling. There are Sasquatch clansmen all over the world. Some call them Yeti, Mystery Apes, Mapinguari, Yowie, Wild Men, Bigfoot... But we are all the same. We travel to other areas to avoid inbreeding, but our race is growing extinct. With the human population explosion and the advances in technology, practically every ten-year-old on the planet has access to a cell phone and video recording devices. Or at least in the US. Sightings are up. It's getting harder and harder to stay hidden. Shifting in downtown Seattle doesn't help things."

Ruby laughed. "I suppose not."

Ethan smiled. "I know it's a lot to take in." He glanced up the staircase then leaned in nearer to whisper to Ruby. "The clan council will have tons of questions. The thief has come forward with a Sasquatch story. The clan won't let it go. They'll interrogate, investigate, and intimidate you, Ruby, until they are sure, absolutely 100 percent sure, you won't breathe a word of what you know or have seen. I'm sorry I dragged you into this. But if we don't do this now, things will only get worse. At least this way is on our terms and not…another way."

Ruby shuddered. "What other way could there be?"

"Best case scenario? If you turn on us, they'll make you into a laughingstock. They'll ruin you, Ruby. Your career. Your life."

"And the worst case scenario?"

Ethan hesitated, not wanting to share the darkest side of his nature and history. "The Sasquatch adults are capable of a powerful supernatural hypnotism that can kill prey outright, or, in lesser intensities, rewire memories into a scrambled chaos, rendering our enemies incapable of spilling centuries of Sasquatch secrets. The clan jokingly refers to it as the Whammy."

"Doesn't sound very funny to me." Ruby chewed on her lower lip. "Secrets like I've already seen? Like you're telling me now?"

Ethan clenched his hands into fists, knowing he was dragging her further into his life. "Yes."

“How do I convince the clan council I won’t talk? Which I won’t, by the way.”

Ethan’s blue eyes locked with hers, the solution coming to his mind seconds before he voiced it aloud. “We convince them it’s already too late. Tell them you’re pregnant with my child and convince them we’re in love.”

Chapter Seven

Holy shit. Holy shit. Holy shit.

So these were her options? Have her life and career ruined, endure a Sasquatch lobotomy, or convince the clan she was pregnant with a secret Sasquatch love child?

Yeah, that all seemed perfectly normal.

Cthulhu, drag me under the sea, now.

Ruby's mind pinged like a marble in a blender. Even if she convinced the clan with this crazy plan, weren't they eventually going realize she wasn't pregnant? That there was no baby? This was a terrible plan, but she wasn't coming up with anything better.

All she wanted to do was go home and cancel her Internet. This entire mess started with that stupid *Daveslist* ad.

She felt the boat slowing, and it began to rock harder in the surf. Ruby pressed her face to the window and spotted the island's dock they were headed for. Two Lummi men waited there, their long black hair giving away their heritage.

"Ruby, come on up," Ethan called through the opening from the deck.

She gathered herself, smoothing her clothing, and wrapped her peacoat tightly around her, tying her belt with trembling hands. Her nausea seemed to worsen upon standing. Regardless of what was to come, she was damned ready to be off this boat. She walked to the back doors and waited.

Ethan offered his hand to steady her as she stepped out onto the back decking. She took his warm hand in hers, and he squeezed gently, reassuring her with a small smile. Instead of releasing her, he tucked their clasped hands into his generous coat pocket, pulling her in close against him.

"Might as well start the show," Ethan said, leaning down to peck her on the cheek. His lips left a warm spot despite the cold wind that had already chilled her to the bone.

February boat rides on the Sound were dicey on good days. The darkening sky to the east said this was not going to be a good day. The wind gusted and Ethan turned her so as to block the gale with his body. Jacob maneuvered the yacht parallel to the crude dock. It was a ridiculously large boat for such a small dock. The men on shore went to work securing the behemoth, like they'd done it before.

"You must be cold, too," Ruby said.

"We run hot. My internal thermostat stays over one hundred degrees. I'm a walking heater."

Ruby resisted the urge to comment on his general hotness. Because, yeah, he was all kinds of hot, and this close to him? He smelled wonderful. Like pine needles and sandalwood.

Jacob joined them on the boarding deck. "Good times."

Ethan squeezed her hand inside his pocket then led her off the boat.

"Mr. Lane, it's been too long since we've seen you. Welcome back," the older Lummi man said.

"Thank you, Vernell," Ethan said.

"How long you staying, Mr. L? You want me to send the girls up to clean your place real quick? Knock down the cobwebs at least?" the younger Lummi man asked.

"No thanks, Henry. We're good."

Henry gave Ruby a long, hard appraisal but didn't comment.

"Full moon tonight," Vernell said.

"Yep." Ethan pulled her along the dock past a half-dozen ten-foot-high totems with the predominate theme of men and other creatures holding long salmon. Jacob stayed behind, talking to Vernell and Henry.

"You have a home here, too?" Ruby asked.

"It's more of an apartment on the east shore of the island, as far away from the casino as possible."

"There's a casino here? How is that safe for you? Won't you be seen if you…change?"

"There are nearly twenty thousand acres of dense forest on the reservation and three roads in by Lummi offices. Most of our residents live along the shoreline. Visitors won't make it far without a tribe member knowing. Trust me. Your presence is being scrutinized as we speak. Poor Jacob is getting the what for back there."

"Why didn't they ask you—or me—who I am?"

"The Lummi are a lot of things, but rude isn't one of them."

"Oh." Ruby pulled her hand free from Ethan's and pushed it into her own pocket.

The wind picked up the ends of her hair and whipped it about her face. She struggled to contain it, twisting it into a bun at the back of her head and tucking it beneath her coat collar.

Ethan approached a small parking lot kiosk and tapped on the sliding window. A man sat inside watching a movie on a tiny laptop computer screen.

"Hey, Ethan. You need your car?"

"I do."

The man handed Ethan a ring with two keys on it. "Good to see you again."

Ethan took the keys. "Thanks."

"It's behind the kiosk, against the fence. I washed it last week for you."

Ethan grimaced. "You didn't have to. But thanks again."

"They seem to like you a lot here," Ruby said as they crossed the lot. "How long has it been since you've been here?"

A dimple in his cheek appeared when he clenched his jaw. "Six months."

"Why so long?"

He chirped open his car locks and looked at her over the roof of the vehicle. "I want to live my life, Ruby. Be a normal guy. I didn't ask for this curse, and I'd give anything to be rid of it. Instead, I've made things worse."

Ethan opened his door then hesitated and walked around to her side. He wrapped his arms around her and leaned in, his lips claiming hers. Her hands slid up and against his ribs, his body firm and strong beneath her touch. Ethan released her and backed away, reaching for her door handle.

"Sorry about that. The parking attendant is watching us. When the tribunal meets, everyone gets a vote."

"So you're campaigning?" she squeaked.

"That and I rudely forgot to get your door for you."

"Oh," was all she could muster, her head still swimming from his unexpected kiss. If it was for show, he was a hell of an actor. And kisser. He closed her door and returned to the driver's side.

He started the car and backed out. Her stomach growled loudly, breaking the uncomfortable silence. "You're hungry?"

"Yes. Sorry."

"Don't be. It's been a long night. I could use some coffee and something more substantial than a cookie myself. There's a café on the way. It's not much to get excited about, but it will do."

"I don't want to be a bother."

"You're not. It's a fifteen minute drive from here. This is all my fault, Ruby. The least I can do is feed you."

Ruby belted in and concentrated on the scenery.

***

Had he lost his ever-loving mind? This was a terrible plan.

Ethan cursed himself for his lame plotting. He was a writer, for God's sake, which was absolutely no help in real life. If his characters misbehaved, he could bend them to his will or kill them off. Real people were much less amenable.

Everything was going to hell. He'd brought Ruby to the island to protect her but, now, it seemed he'd delivered the lamb to slaughter instead. God, he should have run. Should have taken Ruby and run. No way she'd have gone with him, though. She'd only agreed to this excursion because she was still in shock. Their one failed date had ended in a mugging and, technically, kidnapping. He didn't see any way this story ended in "Kids, this is how I met your mother."

They had a day, maybe two, before the tribunal convened and voted. Then they'd carry out whatever punishment they deemed fit. The tribunal council consisted of half Sasquatch and half Lummi members. In his favor, Jacob was a councilman—not in his favor, Elizabeth's father, Joseph, was also on the council. Elizabeth was his Squatch match, or at least would have been if he'd had any interest whatsoever in perpetuating his line.

To say Joseph would be shocked by his surprise faux child would be an understatement. He didn't want to think about what Jacob was going to say.

It was amazing how quickly the lies could add up, but he was backed against a wall. He couldn't see any other way out.

A fake secret baby? A thief with a Sasquatch attack story? And a photographer with potential photos of him shifting?

God help him.

He pulled off the one main road that circled the peninsula and drove into the parking lot of the latest incarnation of the reservation cafés. There would be stares and side chatter about his guest from the regulars.

The show was about to begin. At least he didn't have to worry about that stupid photographer here. If he could garner enough goodwill before the inevitable tribal vote, he could hopefully avoid punishment for Ruby. He'd take whatever they dealt out as long as she was spared.

Ruby was out of the car before Ethan could make his way around to open the door for her.

"You ready for this?" he asked, taking her hand.

"Considering the options you gave me and my current level of hunger? Yes."

He squeezed her hand and led her into the diner.

They took a table on the left, facing the door. Ruby slid into the booth and Ethan followed. He helped her shrug off her jacket then removed his own. The waitress appeared at their table with two full coffee cups before he could pick up the menu.

"Nice to see you, Ethan," she said.

Ethan looked up to see Connie Whitesail. She set the mugs on the table in front of them.

"Heard you were in town." She gave Ruby a once-over. "You two ready to order?"

Ethan eased an arm around Ruby's shoulders and pulled her in close. "I think so. The regular, hon?"

A small smile turned up the corner of Ruby's mouth. "Sure."

"Two orders of biscuits and gravy, please. And a side of hash browns." He gave Connie a wink. "We'll share."

The waitress straightened and sent a quick side-eyed glance toward the kitchen. He could see several of the diners' curious faces reflected in the security mirrors mounted in the corners.

"Coming right up," she said, spinning on her heel and heading off to place their order.

Ethan leaned in and nuzzled Ruby's neck. "Winning Connie over would be a real boon. She's the engine behind 90 percent of the island's gossip chain."

"Only 90?" Ruby scoffed.

"The other 10 percent comes from the marina. Vernell and Henry work fast."

The sound of her laughter filled him with hope. Ethan squeezed her in a side hug, and Ruby tilted her head to rest on his shoulder. The intimate gesture caught him off guard. To anyone in the diner, they appeared every bit the couple he was trying to portray. His heart ached. He tried to convince himself the ache was caused by the deception and not his longing to make the lie so.

Before he could examine the moment further, it was broken when Connie returned with their food.

"You gonna introduce me to your friend, Ethan, or make me find out the hard way?" Connie asked.

"Connie, this is my girlfriend, Ruby." Ethan smiled and watched her face as she processed the reality Ruby was neither Lummi nor a known Squatch match. Every adult on the reservation knew the history and the secret they were all keeping. Ethan's fate and path forward for the next couple of days now lay firmly in the hands of the peninsula's most competent power broker and information wielder.

"Well, it's been a good long time since I saw you smile. Good for you, Ethan. Nice to meet you, Ruby." Connie filled their empty coffee cups first. "Don't be a stranger around here."

He watched Connie walk away in the front window reflection.

"Good?" Ruby asked.

"Very." He gave her another quick peck on the cheek, and color flooded her face. "Eat up."

By the time they finished their meals and at least three refills of coffee, Ethan felt almost human again. He chuckled to himself as they made their way down the block and back to the ferry. Ruby was exhausted, and he decided he could return to the marina convenience store for the groceries they needed after he had her settled in. The store was crude—the locals made the trip to Bellingham once a week or so for "real" shopping, but he could get some basics. Enough for a few days anyway.

He drove toward the cabin.

His mind was so full of tangled thoughts, he missed his driveway. Ethan slammed on the brakes and skidded to a stop then backed up and turned down his mile-long gravel driveway. Driveway may have been a bit generous description. The rain had washed some pretty decent potholes in it while he'd been gone. The Honda dragged its fragile belly along the rough terrain, and Ruby bounced like a rag doll next to him.

She grabbed the Oh Jesus handle and clutched the console for purchase.

"You might need a Jeep or something," she said.

"Sorry."

Trees canopied the driveway all the way down. The forest was so dense on this part of the reservation, the road didn't even appear on Google Earth. Just how he liked it. There were several little homes hidden on the reservation. The Lummi were a sovereign nation but considered the Sasquatch clan their own in all ways so encouraged them to live on the reservation where they were safe and revered. The "apartment" came into view.

"That's a cabin," Ruby said.

"I didn't want to oversell it."

"You didn't."

At less than 450 square feet, it would have been considered a tiny home, he supposed. Certainly it was compared to his Bainbridge place. Honestly, it was a glorified storage barn, modified a bit. The little wood stove gave plenty of heat. Oil lanterns provided light. They did have running water, powered by a couple of solar panels on the roof, and a propane stove and hot water heater for the tiny tub/shower combo.

Rustic came to mind. What the cabin lacked in amenities, it made up for in other comforts, like the bed he'd had delivered after too many nights on the futon, which had finally officially been deemed a full-time couch instead. That bed took up half the cabin, but it was worth it. Nothing much to do out here in the woods for him when he wasn't on the prowl but sleep and read anyway. He'd never had a visitor other than Jacob, who usually slept on his boat.

Ethan counted back in his head. Four times he'd stayed here last year. He dreaded what he'd find inside and already wished there was a fire going for Ruby.

"Home sweet home…again."

Ethan parked at the end of the driveway, still protected from prying eyes by the tree canopy. The pines were tall here, and the log cabin with its green roof was well camouflaged with a window of light peeking through for the solar panels. The cabin was the perfect Squatch pad in every way except he was 99 percent sure the cupboards were completely bare, which made a trip to the Park 'N Shop absolutely necessary.

He wanted to give Ruby a chance to acclimate, and they needed to have a serious getting-to-know-you cramming session before the interrogation began. He knew Jacob would hold that off as long as he could, but it wouldn't be long enough.

He pushed open the unlocked door and batted at the dust motes stirring around his face. The little cabin was dark with the cover of the canopy and the approaching storm.

"Let me get some lights," Ethan said, crossing to his collection of oil lamps.

Ruby pulled back the blinds on the little window by the door and tied them back. "This might help."

It did. She repeated the process with the other two small windows. The largest one took up most of the back wall. She hesitated then crawled up onto the bed, sliding the curtains open until the light poured in.

"That's much better." Ethan lit the lamps and placed them strategically around the cabin. "Heat's next. There's cordwood behind the cabin. I'll bring some in."

"I didn't know you were a lumberjack, too," Ruby teased.

"I'm afraid there's a lot we don't know about one another. I have some useful skills."

"I guess we'll see."

"Make yourself comfortable. Sorry for the crude accommodations."

"It's okay. Feels like the cabins my family used stay in at Chadron State Park." Ruby sat gingerly on the end of the bed with her hands folded in her lap.

"Right, in Nebraska."

"Yes. Do you know it?"

Oh, he knew it. Jacob had taken a cleaner team there in 2006. Luckily, the situation had de-escalated and the Horner Sasquatch patriarch had promised to stop walking around in daylight in full Squatch mode.

"We have a small clan there. Lots of National Forest near the park. Not enough room for more than a family or two, though."

Ethan couldn't stop the smile curling across his face. The little glow of the lantern and the backlight of the window gave Ruby a halo effect all around her long brown curls. She was gorgeous. He'd known it the first time he'd met her in line, but now that he'd had the chance to really see her? God. He couldn't stop staring at her. Besides that, it felt good to be able to talk to someone about all of this. Too bad there was no way it could last.

"I grew up in Alliance, which isn't far from there." Ruby shivered and rubbed her hands up and down her arms.

"Right. Heat. I'm on it."

Ethan made his way to the door and stepped outside to gather wood and his thoughts. They had a lot of ground to cover and little time to get there. But they still needed a few provisions before that could happen.

Chapter Eight

Jacob Chandler made his way through the maze of offices to council Co-President Joseph Ballew's desk. Joseph was the head of Lummi/Sasquatch affairs, and he alone gave the orders for any necessary Sasquatch scrubbings. Jacob had been party to plenty in his life so far, but never in their thirty-five year friendship on behalf of his friend. They'd grown up like brothers. Jacob would make sure things stayed that way. He'd protect Ethan, no matter what it took. Ruby seemed like a nice girl, but she wasn't worth ruining his life over. He'd begged Ethan to abandon his stupid notions of ending the shifts. He had a perfectly good Squatch girl in Elizabeth, right here on the reservation. He'd have been set, but no. Ethan couldn't make himself love her.

Personally, Jacob could live with much less permanent attachments, but Ethan was a happily-ever-after sort of guy. Whatever.

Jacob knocked on Joseph's doorframe, and the man looked up from his laptop screen.

"Thank God. Took you long enough." Joseph pushed his chair back from the desk and rose to shake his hand.

"I came on the boat. From Bainbridge. I brought Ethan back."

"And a lady friend, I hear. What the hell is going on, Jacob?"

"Things went a little sideways. I'm on it. I can get it contained."

"Well, I'd say it's a long ways from contained. You saw the links. Thank God nothing's clear. I swear, when HD thermal security cameras go affordable, we're fucked six ways to Sunday."

Jacob nodded. He wasn't kidding. Ethan had gotten inordinately lucky.

"What happened?" Joseph asked. "The real story, not what I heard on King5."

"Ethan was on a date. They got mugged, and he squatched out. You saw that part. No one was hurt and no other known witness."

"Except the girl, right? The one he's come home with? She saw him attack the mugger?"

"Not exactly."

"Don't make me pry this out of you, Jacob, I know Ethan is your friend, but we can't make this go away without all the information."

"Yes. She's being contained as we speak."

"And how do you figure that? Did she see him shift or not?"

"Yes."

Joseph sighed. "This problem is growing by the second. Anything else I need to know?"

"There's a roommate. She didn't see anything and doesn't know anything but she's adamant about Ruby coming home. It's only a matter of time before she starts making noise. The thief already ransacked their place. I assume he was looking for proof for his story. He stole some electronics. I think he'll be at Ethan's tonight. That's why we came back here first. We only found out about the King5 debacle on the way." Jacob purposely left out the potential snag with the photographer. The last thing he wanted was to add Ethan's pen name and clandestine career to the mix. Not until he had to, anyway.

Joseph flattened his palms across the desk and smoothed one hand back and forth in thought. "Dispatch a team to Ethan's house and wait for him. Has Ruby had contact with the roommate?"

Jacob grimaced. "Yes."

"Unsupervised access?"

"Yes."

"What a clusterfuck. You go to the roommate personally. See what she knows and report back to me by five. I don't want to go into this tribunal committee meeting blinder than I have to. Be thorough, Jacob. You know what we have to lose here."

"I do."

***

Claire paced the apartment. It was way too quiet and way too empty without Ruby. She'd almost called Ruby's parents in Nebraska a dozen times, but what could they do to help, really? And Ruby had insisted she wasn't in danger. Damn thief had taken all of her electronics including their small flat screen television. Everything except her phone, which she'd had with her. She was paralyzed with indecision. Hell, she wasn't sure where they were taking Ruby. Ruby had said she was on a boat. Not helpful. The Sound was lousy with islands. Ruby could be anywhere. Claire absolutely hated feeling helpless, and she was ready to kick some serious ass.

This was all her fault. If she hadn't answered that damn ad and pushed Ruby to meet him, none of this would have happened. None of it.

A knock at her door sent her half out of her skin. She didn't own a firearm. What she did own was a can of bear spray from hiking the many trails near their home, and she knew exactly where it was. Claire raced to the bedroom and grabbed the can from her nightstand, clicking the trigger over to fire. Not that she expected the thief to return…or knock, but who the hell knew what was going on anymore. The last thing she was going to be was a victim. Now or ever.

Claire peeked through the peephole, one hand on the chain and the other on the bear spray. A strange but well-dressed man stood outside her door. Hard to get perspective on his size through the distorted carnival glass-bubble viewer, but two things were clear: he was hot and he was pissed.

Another impatient knock spurred her to action.

"Who are you?" Claire asked through the door.

The man stared straight at the peephole. "Jacob Chandler. I'm a friend of Ethan's…and Ruby's, sort of… I need to talk to you about their…situation."

Ah, the man Ruby had mentioned, Ethan's friend. Now they were getting somewhere. Still, he was a stranger, and she didn't have to make it easy for him.

"So talk."

"It's a bit more delicate than that, Miss…?"

"You came to my house. I think you know who I am."

"Trying to be polite."

"Try harder."

The man hung his head for the briefest of moments, betraying his irritation. "I can't talk about this through the door, Miss Myles."

"Are you the guy who took her from Bainbridge on his boat?"

"Yes."

"What was she wearing?"

"What?"

"What. Was. She. Wearing?" Was this guy slow or annoying on purpose?

"Um, some kind of sweater dress and tights?"

"What color was her coat?"

"Purple?"

"Fuchsia. Close enough."

Claire pondered. She really wanted to know where Ruby was. This guy could get her there. No—this guy *would* get her there. Tucking the can of bear spray into her waistband, she slid the chain, unbolted the door, and opened it to six and a half feet of yummy. Jacob's dark wool jacket stretched tight across his broad shoulders. Soft denim jeans ended in black boots. Then she dragged her gaze back up him. His bright-green eyes had to be the result of contact lenses. Normal people didn't have eyes that color.

Vain.

She already disliked him. In her experience, guys who looked this good had the personalities of rocks. Probably a gym rat to get an upper body like that. He was well put together and his perfectly calculated amount of beard scruff said, *I'm sexy but rugged.*

He could sell that crap all day long. As far as she was concerned, he was a means to an end: getting Ruby home.

Judgy much?

Whatever.

"May I come in?" he asked.

How long had she stood there staring at him like an idiot? *Good Lord.* "Yes."

"Thank you." He walked past her, pulling off his gloves. Jacob did a quick and somewhat rude appraisal of their front room. "I see the thief did some redecorating?"

"We don't live like slobs if that's what you're insinuating. I haven't had a chance to tidy up yet. I'm still waiting for a detective to come by so I can make a report."

He walked over and lingered at their bookshelf. "So no report's been filed yet?"

Ruby hesitated. Why was it any of his damned business? He wasn't a cop. "Are you a cop?"

Jacob spared her a sideways glance. The corner of his mouth curled up into a half smile. "Do I look like a cop?"

Ruby looked him up and down in an intentional assessment. "Absolutely not. You looked like a hipster."

His smile vanished, and he rubbed his brow. "I'm a doctor, actually."

No way. Nothing about this guy said doctor. He had to be lying. "Really? So I have this mole…"

"Not a dermatologist. Sorry."

Figured.

"Why are you here, Mr. Chandler? And where is my friend?"

"Ruby needs a few things. Ethan was under the impression you'd packed a bag for her? I'm here to pick it up."

"I packed a bag. But I'll be the one to deliver it to her. You can take me there."

"I don't think so. This is a big enough mess already."

"Let me uncomplicate it for you. Take me to Ruby, and we'll be out of your hair. End of story."

Jacob gave her a hard look. There was no give in this man. He was all business and hard edges. A little vein above his temple pulsed.

"What did Ruby tell you? When she called you from my boat?"

"Not nearly enough. Mostly that Ethan was worried the thief would try his house next. She said he had a safer place they could go for a few days. I do not understand why he couldn't bring her home first. The thief's already cleaned us out. No reason for him to return."

Jacob continued around the room, thumbing through some old newspapers on her ottoman. "What did she tell you about Ethan?"

"You mean her kidnapper?"

"Did she call him her kidnapper?"

Busted.

"No. Of course not. I think she still likes the guy even after all this mess. He must be something special is all I have to say." Claire's annoyance grew with each object Jacob picked up for inspection. "You know, you're a rude guest, poking around like you own the place. Where do you practice medicine exactly?"

"Private practice," Jacob said. "Have you seen the news today?"

"No, Captain Observant. Do you see a television here? Hello, gone."

"You haven't been online either?"

"I've been busy. What are you really asking me? Be clear."

“I don’t think you need to file that report. Ethan is happy to compensate you for your missing electronics. Make a list. I’ll take it with me and have a check cut. You’ll have it by the end of the day.”

Claire laughed. “Why would he do that? How will the police ever stop this guy if I don’t at least file a report? In fact, in twelve more hours, I’m going to file a missing person’s report on Ruby if she isn’t home safe and sound. Tell him that. Or, better yet, call him and let me tell him.”

“No cell phone. His phone was stolen as well.”

“Well, *your* phone wasn’t stolen. I have your number. I captured it when Ruby called. And now I have your name. If you don’t take me with you so I can bring Ruby home, I’ll not only file the burglary report, but I’ll file a kidnapping report.” Claire grabbed her coat and purse from the chair near the door, slipping the bear spray into her coat pocket. “And you can bet I’ll be sure to mention that Jacob Chandler and Robin Woodring were the perpetrators.”

***

Jacob drove much faster than was prudent along the I-5 back to the reservation. Things had not gone as he’d hoped. Ruby’s roommate was incorrigible. While he didn’t think she had any knowledge of the Sasquatch problem, her threat of exposing Ethan’s pseudonym and sending the police after them to investigate a kidnapping allegation was enough she needed to be neutralized. Somehow, he doubted she was the sort of girl who let things go. Claire fumed defiantly in the seat beside him, twisting her long blonde braid through her fingers repeatedly. It was driving him crazy.

“Please stop that,” he said.

“Stop what?” she snapped.

“The hair. It’s…distracting.”

“The sooner we get to Ruby, the sooner you won’t have to be distracted by my hair. Win/win.”

No, there would be no winning here. She was going to be a problem. But, at least now, she’d be a problem at the reservation where he could contain her instead of a wildcard stirring up more trouble in town. He’d have to put her on ice until after the tribunal. The results of the vote would determine how he’d have to deal with her.

One more loose end to tie up tonight after the committee meeting. His team should already be getting into place.

It was going to be a very long night.

Chapter Nine

Ruby stood inches away from the woodstove, her hands hovering over the cast iron top, slowly thawing her icy fingers. She was still dressed for a date night, not the Arctic. Ethan had started the fire then left for groceries. Now she was stranded in the cabin, alone. Without her phone, she had no idea what time it was. It felt like late afternoon at least, maybe later. Icy rain began to pelt the metal roof, and she snuggled closer to the stove.

Claire was probably going out of her mind.

When her fingers finally regained some dexterity, she began to peruse the bookshelf. There were no Woodring books here, which seemed odd to her. What he did have was an ample collection of Sasquatch lore. Sadly, no *Care and Feeding of Sasquatch* or *Sasquatch For Dummies*. Nothing that helpful. She plucked a volume from the case and curled up on the bed, kicking her shoes to the floor and dragging a super-fleecy blanket over her body. There was plenty of light now with the oil lamps and the window behind her. She settled in to read a purportedly nonfiction book called *Sasquatch Science*.

Expecting to find the choice hokey and ridiculous, she was surprised by the number and global range of the reports of such creatures, just as Ethan had told her. Of course, he'd probably read all these books. If she hadn't seen him change before her eyes, she'd have assumed he was regurgitating factoids from his own research instead of his life experience. It was all fascinating, but the longer she read, the heavier her eyelids grew. Finally warm, she drifted off to sleep to the steady patter of ice pelting the roof.

***

My God, is everyone on the island shopping today?

Ethan sped the tiny grocery basket to the checkout, trying to avoid any more eye contact. He'd already been stopped three times while gathering a few snacks and coffee. Lots of coffee. The Ruby-is-my-girlfriend campaign was exhausting, and he'd only been at it a few hours. Word he was back on the island, and with a friend, had already spread like wildfire. Mercifully, no one had asked about the incident downtown, but he was foolish to think most of them didn't already know. How long before Elizabeth found out? She taught second grade at the elementary school. Maybe she wouldn't hear through the island grapevine for a while at least. He prayed she didn't come to the cabin. Four hours. He'd been on the island four freakin' hours, and he was right back into the thick of things.

He'd have to try to cram in as much time with Ruby as he could before he had to leave to run tonight. He hoped he could make it until midnight.

The full moon might not give him a choice. The higher it rose, the stronger it pulled at him, regardless of the weather. He paid for his groceries and headed to the car. Ice peppered him as he pushed the cart across the uneven parking lot. He tossed the bags into the backseat and climbed in, slamming the door on his jacket. He was cold and dripping wet. What a miserable day. He dreaded running tonight. His normally high temperature wasn't helping him much right now. Without his squatch hair, he was almost as cold and soggy as the next guy.

Thoughts of Ruby curled up by his fire in various stages of undress flitted unbidden through his mind. He was a mess. Hopefully, the run tonight would restore him to factory settings, and he could focus on the task at hand: getting Ruby safely home and back to her life. He knew it was the right thing and the only thing that could happen. So why did it seem less and less desirable to do the right thing?

His dash clock read 4:45 p.m. Daylight was nearly gone. There were only a few short hours before he had to leave her and go fulfill his biological needs. He floored the Honda and sped toward the cabin.

***

Faraday stood in the cold, nervously flipping his phone over and over in his coat pocket as he waited at an abandoned industrial park for Garret Decker. He'd insisted the man not bring his ridiculously conspicuous van. Suddenly, he had a whole new appreciation for the folks he stalked and photographed. This was the least visible place he could think of to meet the hunter. The last thing he wanted was to get scooped. He and Decker had mutual interest in this particular case. Decker was a true believer. He wasn't in it for the money. His reality show barely garnered enough advertising revenue to keep it limping along. Still, this case could help them both. But, even with the photos, they needed a live Bigfoot for the final, undeniable proof. They needed Ethan Lane. And Faraday couldn't do that alone.

Decker had a team of hunters he could enlist to help. All Faraday had to do was point them in the right direction and then release his photos as it all came to a head. Timing would be everything.

A grey sedan pulled around the end of one long building and Faraday tensed. The driver flashed his lights twice. Decker. He walked out of the shadow of the building to meet him.

Decker pulled alongside him. "Mr. Faraday?"

"Mr. Decker. Thanks for coming. This is a delicate situation. I'm sorry I couldn't tell you more. In my business, as in yours, however, a picture is worth a thousand words. Yes? Let's say, these…may be worth significantly more." Faraday extracted his phone from his pocket. Decker reached for it. "Look with your eyes. I'll hold it, thanks."

Decker chuckled. "So that's how it is, huh?"

"Yes."

"Alright, then, show me."

Faraday pulled up the first photo of Lane striking the attacker and slowly swiped left, the scene unfolding like a cartoon flipbook. Mild annoyance gave way to interest and finally rapt study as Decker watched.

Decker's rounded eyes then focused hard at the final frame. "Where the hell did you get these?"

Faraday started to pull the phone out of the window, but Decker's hand latched onto his arm. "Not yet. Blow that last one up, please."

Faraday did. Decker pressed his face close to the screen. "You've Photoshopped these."

"I haven't."

"Where did you get them?"

"I took them. Last night. In downtown Seattle."

Decker sat up straight in the driver's seat, the pieces clicking together for him. "The sighting on King5?"

"Yes."

"You witnessed it?"

"The entire thing."

"I'm going to need to authenticate those photos."

"You're not getting my photos, but I know where you can find the man."

Decker nodded. "Show me the way."

***

Ruby woke with a start when the cabin door slammed against the wall and a strong, frigid wind slapped her in the face. She bolted upright in bed, scrambling away from the doorway and whatever danger was about to befall her. Seconds later, Ethan pushed his way inside, his arms and hands loaded with white plastic grocery bags. He kicked a cooler along the hardwood floor then hooked his foot around the door and shoved it closed behind him, sealing out the elements. Ethan's clothes dripped. Somehow, soaked to the bone, he sent a tremor of attraction through her. He shook his head hard, sending little icy bits flying. One thin icicle plopped from his elbow to the floor beneath him, joining the ever-growing puddle on the floor.

"You're soaked to the bone," Ruby said, dislodging herself from the tangled fleece blanket.

"The storm's really picked up. I'm not looking forward to being out in it later." Ethan deposited his sacks on the small dining table. Groceries tumbled out of the unstructured bags. A can of Italian tomatoes rolled to the edge and fell toward the floor. Ethan snatched it before it landed and set it upright with the rest of the bounty.

Ruby padded over, careful to avoid the puddles. "What can I do to help?" Her stomach growled loudly. Again. "So sorry. Please excuse me."

Ethan sent her a weary smile. "I'm sorry it took me so long. I'll make it up to you. I'm going to make us some dinner. God, seems like all we've done is eat."

"In my defense, brunch was several hours ago. I like all three meals." She laughed.

"Good to know." He struggled to unpack the bags, shivering as he continued to drip, drip, drip.

"Here, let me do this. You should get out of those wet clothes and warm up," Ruby said, taking cans from his icy cold hands. "Your hands are freezing."

"Thanks. I think I'll do that. Don't worry about the cooler. It will be fine. I'll get things started in a few minutes. I hope you like Italian."

"Italian is my favorite." Ruby smiled, barely resisting the urge to sweep the wet hair from his face.

Ethan turned and shed his wool coat, hanging it on the large iron hook on the back of the entry door. It sagged, heavy with water. His dress shirt was soaked through and clung to his strong chest, accentuating his pecs and biceps. Ruby tried not to stare, but damn. And damn.

He began unbuttoning his shirt as he moved toward the tiny bathroom then backed up and opened a skinny armoire to remove dry clothes from the shelves there. Everything was stacked in neat piles; T-shirts, flannels, jeans. Not at all what she would have expected him to favor. He disappeared behind the closing bathroom door, and Ruby heard the water turn on and then the shower.

Ruby shivered. She wasn't sure if it was the lingering cold or the thought of Ethan undressing on the other side of that thin door. Back to the task at hand. Unpacking.

She emptied the dozen bags and wadded them up into a ball, stuffing them into one then neatly organized the groceries on the tiny table: tomatoes, mushrooms, a baguette, pasta. Tiptoeing carefully to the cooler, she opened it and peered inside: Italian sausages, a chunk of parmesan cheese…wine. Her stomach growled again. Yes, this would do.

Some reports from her earlier reading had said Sasquatches were omnivores, others reported them as carnivorous. As reluctant to embrace his condition as he seemed, she'd worried maybe he was vegan. That would have been a deal breaker. Ruby chuckled to herself. Yeah, *that* would have been the deal breaker? What was wrong with her?

Regardless, it appeared she'd be eating in the near future, which did not displease her. Not at all.

She did a quick kitchen inventory: one big pot, a skillet, and an apartment-sized two-burner stove with oven. A gas oven. She turned the burner knob to ignite and snapped the dial several times. Nada. Pilot light was likely out. Hmmm.

Sorting through a row of cabinet drawers, she found a long lighter and half crawled inside the tiny oven searching for the extinguished pilot to re-ignite. The lighter sparked, and the pilot lit with a whoosh, scaring her and causing her to hit her head on the oven wall. A little squeak escaped her, quickly followed by a chuckle. From behind her.

"Oh." She jumped up, hands trembling, and slammed the oven door closed.

"You okay?" Ethan asked.

Her jaw dropped. Ethan stood way too near her now, his bare feet peeking out from soft denim jeans and his broad shoulders bathed in a dusty-blue and cream plaid flannel shirt. His beard was fuller than when they'd left and a tuft of chest hair curled over the top of the wife beater undershirt stretched across his chest. The open flannel invited her to take the two steps necessary to run her hands under the hem of that cotton undershirt and up, across his hot, solid…

Ack!

"You look better," she said, trying not to stare.

"Feel better. Thanks for lighting the pilot. You're pretty handy."

"I have some skills, too," she said, immediately regretting the entendre.

A slow smile pulled at the corner of his mouth, deepening the same tiny dimple she'd seen earlier.

"I'll take over," he said, reaching above her head and pulling the pasta pot from the hook.

"We can do it together. I'm not entirely helpless, you know."

"I can see that."

Ethan towered over her now. She could feel the heat radiating off him, creating a snuggly cloud of warmth, drawing her nearer. He extended his arms on either side of her, trapping her against the sink. He set the big pot on the cabinet to her left and leaned in, hovering inches from her face. She closed her eyes, waiting for the kiss. Instead, she heard the rattle of metal to her right and saw he'd retrieved the skillet as well.

He set it on the cabinet, too, but lingered there. Tension coiled inside her. She wanted him to kiss her. Right here. Right now. Not because people were watching and they needed to put on a show. She wanted him to kiss her because *he* wanted to. He searched her face, clearly undecided despite her rapidly increasing heart rate and breathing. He had to see she was waving him in, right?

Ethan pulled back. "You can fill this pot with water, then. There's some kosher salt in that top cabinet."

Right. Back to business.

Ruby did as instructed and tried to calm her galloping heart. Why hadn't he kissed her?

Good grief.

Ethan set the skillet on the stovetop and lit the burner. The sausages sparked to life, popping and sizzling. Ethan stirred in the canned mushrooms and crumbled the meat as it cooked.

They worked side by side, and the immediate tension drained but was replaced with embarrassment. Of course he hadn't kissed her. He probably wanted her out of his hair as quickly as possible so he could get back to writing…and his life. He probably regretted going out with her in the first place. Probably would have never called for a second date. She was an inconvenience.

Well, she'd be gone as soon as she could be. She had a life, too. Pathetic as it was.

“Would you mind opening these?” Ethan asked, pushing two cans of stewed Italian tomatoes her way. “The opener is in that far right drawer.”

She ripped open the drawer and rummaged around until she found the manual opener then went to savagely hacking at the first can. She twisted the tiny key dial around and around and around, peeling little bits of the paper label into a pile of kindling on the counter.

Feeling Ethan’s eyes on her, she glanced up to catch his puzzled expression.

“Everything okay?” he asked while stirring the sausages.

“Peachy.”

“You don’t seem peachy. You seem…pissed.”

“Nope.”

“Okay. Well, then. Tell me more about yourself. The tribunal will want to talk to us separately. To be sure we aren’t fleecing them. We need to cover as much ground as possible before that happens. Tell me more about yourself. Does your family know what’s going on now? Here?”

“No. Claire wouldn’t call them unless it was absolutely necessary. I didn’t feel like it was when I talked to her.” Ruby paused. “Was I wrong?”

“No. This will all be over in a couple of days. I promise.”

“Great.”

The pasta water began boiling. Ethan reached over and turned down the burner. He drained the sausage grease into one of the empty mushroom cans then poured in the tomatoes to cook down. The little house smelled wonderful, and Ruby’s stomach took on a life of its own, grumbling and complaining to be filled.

Ethan searched through a little spice rack on the back of the cabinet door and shook in oregano, basil, and thyme. When the sauce had cooked down, he dug through the cooler, pulled out a little container of heavy cream, and poured half of it into the sauce as well.

"Would you open the wine?" Ethan asked, handing her the corkscrew.

"Sure." Ruby took the bottle and scooted down the counter a bit while Ethan worked.

She looked at the label. *God Only Knows God Only Knows God Only Knows* repeated across the face of the Grenache. Well, wasn't that the truth?

Struggling with the corkscrew, she finally got it started and twisting down. She folded the little metal hooks over the lip of the bottle, but couldn't clamp it down to extract the cork.

"May I help you?" Ethan asked, wiping his hands on a dishtowel.

Slightly miffed at her inability, she handed him the bottle, and he pulled the cork straight out with a satisfying pop. He poured a third of the bottle of dark-red liquid into the sauce then reached up for two glasses, which he filled. He handed one to Ruby.

"I've never seen this wine," she said.

"It was one of Washington's best in 2014. Pricier than I wanted, but the choices at the little store are limited. Cheap and expensive are the two options."

"I can't say I'd have known the difference. I'm not much of a drinker."

"Give it a try."

Ruby took a sip. Then another. "It tastes like olives. And flowers."

Ethan's eyebrows rose in surprise. "Yes. Anything else?

"Salt?"

"Saline. You may have a natural palate for wine."

Ruby shrugged. "Skills…remember?"

Ethan took a long drink from his own glass, swirling it in his mouth before swallowing. "Our next date should be to a wine tasting."

Ruby pulled down another huge gulp, nearly choking on it. "Will there be a second date? I thought you were ready to be rid of me."

Ethan stopped stirring the sauce and looked straight at her. "I want nothing of the sort, Ruby. What I want is what's best for you. I want you to be safe and have a happy life. I don't think I'm the guy who can give that to you. Not after what happened."

"The mugging could have happened to anyone. It could have happened no matter who I was with."

"The mugging wasn't what I'm worried about. I could have hurt you...when I…changed."

"Have you hurt people before?"

Ethan's brows knitted in consternation. "No. But that doesn't mean it couldn't happen. We lose control when we shift. If we avoid it for too long, it gets harder and harder to control. Regular shifting alleviates the distress of the action and allows us to keep more of our human mind and nature intact. I hadn't shifted in so long. If Jacob hadn't shown up when he did…"

Ruby pressed her hand flat against Ethan's chest, his heat radiating through the thin layer of cotton. "Nothing bad happened."

"Why aren't you more upset about this? About…me?" Ethan asked, not making eye contact with her.

"I'm not afraid of you."

"Maybe you should be."

Chapter Ten

Ethan couldn't concentrate on his food. He thought about how much he wanted to kiss Ruby…among other things he'd like to do to her. He'd have been a lot better off if he'd stopped at the first bottle of wine. He hadn't. As soon as he shifted, the wine would be a nonissue, but that was still a few hours away and until then, he was trapped in a twenty-by twenty-two-foot cabin with a woman he wanted to strip down and worship more and more with each glass he drank.

Focus, Ethan.

He sat on the futon next to Ruby. They'd dragged it nearer the stove to stay warm. They had a lot more ground to cover and eight fewer hours to do it in. His afternoon with Ruby had been very enjoyable. They'd talked and talked, drinking wine by the wood stove, her snuggled in his blanket. The whole situation felt downright domestic. Yet…his wild side pulled at him. Jacob's suppressant was a very temporary solution and had worn off hours ago. The cabin had begun to darken. One oil lamp near the bed and the sparks of the fire through the glass stove front bathed the room and Ruby in a soft, warm glow that did nothing to extinguish his raging libido. Ruby looked like a porcelain angel, her soft brown hair falling in a wave down her breasts and curling at the ends.

"Ethan? Are you listening?"

He pulled himself from his mulling. "Sorry. What did you say?"

"I asked why you don't want anyone to know about your writing."

"Right. I'm sure that seems trivial, considering everything else. Have you read any of Robin Woodring's books?"

"You mean *your* books," Ruby corrected.

"Right. It seems weird talking about it in the first person. My books."

"Yes. A few," Ruby said.

"Did you have a favorite?"

Ruby blushed. "*Goodwin Hollow*."

"Ah, the shifter book. Yes. Perfect example. That book is exactly why I want to keep my real career a secret. If you substitute Sasquatch for every time the word werewolf was said or thought in the story, you'll have a pretty good picture of what it's like to be a Squatch and to shift."

Ruby shuddered. "But that was a horror story."

"Exactly. I still can't believe no one on the reservation has ever mentioned it. It was my first book actually. I published it third, but I wrote it first. I was hesitant to send it out into the world. I was afraid it was more exposé than fiction and everyone would catch on. But, with the rise of horror and paranormal fiction, it blended in. It got picked up by Miramax for the movie and then everything exploded. I kept my 'day job,' which actually became my side hustle, and here I am. Saddled with two ginormous secrets I can't tell anyone."

"Except me."

Ethan looked down, studying his hands nervously. "Except you."

"What's the worst that would happen if the clan found out about your writing?"

"I'm not sure."

"Would they…kill you?"

Ethan considered her question. It wasn't the first time he'd asked himself the same thing. He didn't want to think things would go that far, but euthanasia was a very real option. Protecting the clan's secrets was paramount for their continued survival. Or so they continued to believe. There were other enforcement options.

"Probably not. There are so few of us now. They wouldn't want to risk extinction by killing off any of our own unless someone couldn't shift out of Squatch mode anymore and went on some sort of rampage."

Ruby sat forward on the futon, leaning close to him. "That could happen?"

"It has before. There have been a few unfortunate instances in the past. One crazed Sasquatch can do a lot of damage." Ethan paused, deciding whether to continue. "Remember the Donner Party?"

Ruby blanched. "The pioneers who were stranded in the Sierra Nevada's in the 1800s and became cannibals? They were Sasquatches?"

"No. But there was a clan nearby. They were hungry and stayed in Squatch mode trying to survive. It was a long winter. For everyone."

"Oh."

Silence filled the room again. Ruby's hand pressed against his leg. "You're not like that, Ethan."

"But I could be."

Her hand gripped his thigh, sending a bolt straight to his groin. His dick hardened immediately. God, how long had it been since he'd been with a woman? Elizabeth's face popped into his head. Yeah, that he didn't need. Nothing wrong with Elizabeth. She was a wonderful girl. But being with her had been a mistake he was still trying to live down. That night with Elizabeth had been the last time he'd been on the reservation. So, yeah, six months ago.

Six really long months.

"How have you all managed to stay hidden so long, Ethan? Even with the help of Natives, it seems impossible there's never been one of you captured or killed."

Ethan nodded, expecting the question. "Plenty of us have been caught, temporarily, and too many have been killed through the years. Our one self-preserving mechanism is that when we die, we automatically shift back to our primary human form. We have years of evolution to thank for diluting the magic. Centuries ago, it could have gone either way. Now, if someone kills us in Squatch form, they'll never have a Sasquatch body to hold as proof. What they will have is a dead human body and a ridiculous story they can't prove."

"Except for the DNA? Right?"

"That's only been an issue the past decade or so, but yes. Eventually, questions could arise around our DNA if it were ever tested. The witness/suspect would have to be extremely compelling, however, to convince anyone to proceed with testing of that nature in a murder trial. I don't think law enforcement is ready to go down that rabbit hole yet."

"You're never really safe, are you?"

"No."

Ruby's hand rose to caress his beard, drawing his gaze back to her. He hated his scruffiness but couldn't control it at this point. He'd be shaving hourly to maintain a smooth face, and since she already knew…

His heartbeat picked up, and all of his good intentions evaporated at her touch. Ethan leaned in and pressed his lips to Ruby's. Her breath caught, and her hands wound around the back of his neck, pulling him nearer in an urgent kiss. Ethan slid one arm under her blanket and around the small of her back, drawing her body along his until they lay together on the narrow futon. The fire cracked and popped behind the glass of the wood stove, and ice pelted the metal roof at a furious pace that seemed to match the beating of his own heart.

Ethan drew back, catching his breath. "Ruby, I don't know if we should be doing this."

"We're just kissing," she offered, smoothing his hair from his forehead.

"Yeah. But I want to do a lot more." Ethan struggled to regain his control.

"I'm not stopping you."

Great Spirit! Green lights all the way. God help me.

His body won the internal battle he'd been fighting, sending his brain on vacation for a while. Ethan growled and kissed his way down the long, sensuous line of Ruby's throat. She squirmed beneath him, struggling under the thick, fleecy blanket. There was way too much material between them. Ethan rose up from the futon and began to unwrap her from the covering. Her hands slid up his torso beneath his flannel while he struggled, distracting him further and leaving a trail of goose bumps along his flesh that had nothing to do with the temperature.

Finally untangled, he ripped the blanket from her and tossed it toward the bed. Stretching his body across hers, he covered her, holding his full weight from her. He captured her mouth with his, and his tongue teased and explored hers in increasingly urgent thrusts and parries. His erection jutted forward as he settled between her legs. Ruby's hands slid around to his lower back and beneath his jeans' waistband ever so slightly, urging his hips against hers. Her legs parted, and he sank down into the vee of her legs, exactly where he'd longed to be but still with far too many layers of cloth between them.

Ethan reached down beneath her dress, pushing it up over her hips and leaving one less barrier. His hand skimmed across her thick cotton tights and cupped her core, sending more bolts of longing to his groin. He could feel her hardened nub through her underwear and tights. He rubbed, slowly at first then faster, until Ruby began to squirm and mewl, her sounds of pleasure exciting him further.

Ethan stopped abruptly and looked down at her. "Let's move this to the bed."

Ruby bit her lip and nodded, her chest rising and falling with rapid breaths.

Ethan rose and scooped her up in one swift motion then carried her to the bed. He stood her carefully beside him then yanked back the coverings to expose the burgundy sheets below. He held her face in his hands, rubbing his thumbs across her cheekbones, and bent to kiss her again, slow and deep.

"You are so beautiful," Ethan said.

Ruby blushed and tried to look away.

"Don't do that. It's true," he continued.

He grasped the hem of her sweater dress and eased it upward. Ruby raised her arms so he could draw it over her head. Her black bra and tights remained. Ethan slid his thumbs beneath the band of her tights and ran them around her waist. Ruby's hands closed around his and pushed them down. Ethan knelt in front of her and watched her face as he worked the tights to her ankles then off each foot.

Ruby's fingers wound through his hair. He pressed his face to her black panties and inhaled. Her scent reawakened his baser animal instincts that had nothing to do with being a Sasquatch but everything to do with being a man. He tugged her waistband with his teeth until she withdrew her touch from his hair and began pushing the offending clothing down herself.

"In a hurry," Ethan chuckled.

"Yes," Ruby insisted, kicking out of her panties.

Ethan smiled and lowered his face to her exposed mound. Soft brown curls sprang in an inch-wide strip down the center; everywhere else, she was bare. Her thighs pressed together, leaving a small, heart-shaped gap he longed to fill with his tongue. He ran his palms up both legs from ankle to hip then cupped each ass cheek, kneading the firm rounded flesh and pulling her mound against his face. His nose pressed into her curls and his tongue pushed into the gap, darting in and out, brushing the bottom of her fleshy lips.

Ruby shivered and gooseflesh rose across her thighs and legs as he plummeted in and out of the gap. Keeping a firm grip on her ass, he gained a steady rhythm. Ruby parted her legs, giving him better access.

"No." Ethan continued in his slow torturous assault.

Ruby stiffened beneath his hold, and he guessed she was close to orgasm. He rose to his full height and took her mouth again, letting her taste her sweet flavor.

Ethan toed her feet apart with his own and reached to cup her core again, letting his middle finger slip into her to the first knuckle then curling it upward. He repeated the action, dipping into and out of her slick entrance ever so slightly. Ruby's knees began to buckle, and he steadied her, his finger sliding deeper into her as he held her firmly.

"Easy there." Ethan turned her and eased her back onto the bed.

She scrambled backward on her elbows and spread her legs, inviting him to continue. A sly smile curled up the corners of her mouth, and her eyes flashed in the firelight. Ethan unbuttoned his jeans, and Ruby traced the toes of her foot up his leg and across his bulging cock. Her foot flattened and pushed against him, rocking him ever so slightly.

"Shirts off. All of it. Off," she demanded.

Bossy little thing.

Ethan hesitated. "I'm pretty, um…"

"What?" Ruby asked.

"Hairy."

"Lucky for you I happen to like hairy men."

Ethan hoped she wasn't saying that to make him feel better. He wasn't exactly a beast. Not yet anyway. He never grew hair on his back, thank God. At least not until he squatched out. But his chest was definitely covered. As were…other areas. If a guy believed the movies and media, women only liked bare, athletic boy/men. Of course, the Sasquatch women didn't mind, but he wasn't interested in them. He wanted Ruby.

Her toes kneaded at his erection through the denim.

Apparently, she wanted him as well.

Ethan shrugged off the flannel shirt and let it drop to the floor. He grasped the bottom of the tank and peeled it up and over his head in a swift motion so he could catch her eyes and gauge her reaction.

Ruby gave him a slow half smile as her gaze roamed across his torso then she shifted and crawled toward him like a cat. Her heels curled up behind her ass, she arched and ran her hands up his chest and across his pecs, through the forest of reddish-brown hair there. She traced her palms across his abs down to his open jeans, pushing the denim down past his Adonis belt.

Her thumbs traced the muscles there, sliding along the grooves until…

Ethan caught her hands in his and held them while he toed out of his jeans, kicking them out of the way. His soldier stood long and straight in front of him, twitching slightly to the right in her direction, like a divining rod searching for water. He held both of her wrists in his hand and pushed her back onto the bed. If she touched his cock, it was all over.

Nuzzling his beard against her neck, he started working his way back down her body with slow, wet kisses until he reached her peaked nipples. Ruby's legs wrapped around his thighs, urging him closer, but he held his weight off her body as best he could. Her hips rose off the bed with her efforts to pull him tighter to her. Her smooth body slid against his, threatening to spark a fire between them. Ethan kissed lower and lower until he was returned to her core. He teased at her nub, flicking his tongue back and forth as it grew as impossibly hard as his own cock. Pushing two fingers into her, he pumped them in and out then bent to suck at the clit, rolling it gently between his teeth as he worked.

Ruby's breathing hastened. Little grunts and moans escaped her in puffs, and she fisted the sheets. Untangling her legs, she anchored her feet flat on the bed as she achieved release, crying out some unintelligible plea. Her tensed body quivered and pulsed for several long seconds before relenting into boneless repose, one arm flung across her eyes, the other hand still gripping the sheet.

Ethan eased up beside her and pulled her around until he spooned her from behind then drew the covers over them to warm her.

"Oh God," Ruby said, many minutes later. "That was…I don't know what that was, but it was wonderful."

"Hmm…yes. It was." He kissed the back of her neck.

Ruby pushed back against him, spreading her legs enough his cock sprang between them before he could pull back.

"Ruby, I don't have a condom. We'll have to avoid penetration, I'm afraid."

"Are you healthy? I mean, other than the Sasquatch thing. I can't catch that, right? Anything else I need to know about? Health-wise?" Ruby asked, squeezing her thighs around his engorged erection.

"No. I mean…" His mind refused to engage. All he could think of was how warm and good his cock felt right where it was and how much better it would feel a few inches north. "No. You can't catch being a Sasquatch. It's not like getting bitten and becoming a werewolf. You're born one or you aren't." Ruby wiggled her tight ass, and he nearly lost what was left of his worthless mind. "Ah…I…what was the other question?"

"Do you have a clean bill of health? No STDs or other weirdness?"

"Absolutely nothing to worry about, other than pregnancy." Which everyone would think he'd already done this time tomorrow.

"Then what are you waiting for? I have an IUD. We're golden."

"That's very progressive for a Midwestern girl, isn't it?"

"Claire educated me on its merits. I guess I'll owe her one, or twenty." Ruby released her thigh grip around his cock and readjusted.

"As will I." Ethan eased the head of his penis into her wet channel.

"Don't tease me. I know there's more than that."

His control broke. He rolled Ruby over on her stomach and lifted her hips, pushing her to her knees, so he could mount her from behind. He positioned the head of his erection at her entrance and, before he could take action, she pressed back against him to full penetration. Ethan threw his head back and gritted his teeth as she constricted around him. He could feel the tendons along his neck bulging with the strain then he began to stroke in and out of her impossibly tight channel.

Three, four, five strokes were all he lasted before erupting into her. His fingers curled around her hips, digging into her flesh as he wrung out the last possible shiver of orgasm before collapsing beside her. She rolled around to face him and snuggled in close, absorbing his body heat like a cat in the sun. He wrapped his arms around her and breathed into her hair, his eyelids growing heavier. He had no idea what time it was, but it was completely dark outside. He knew he should get up, out of bed, and seek out Jacob before he had to run tonight, but he couldn't bring himself to leave Ruby's side. Closing his eyes for a moment, he savored her company.

This is what normal felt like. What it *could* feel like. What he'd never have again.

Chapter Eleven

Jacob left Ruby's pissed-off roommate locked in the hull bedroom of his boat. Granted, it was a damn nice bedroom, but he was 99 percent certain it wouldn't be when he returned. The one small above-water portal window was six inches thick. He wasn't worried about her wiggling through it. One door led to the upper level, but it bolted from the outside as well as the inside. A precaution he'd added some time ago. He grimaced when he considered what she might do to all of his bar glasses. He had to keep her on ice until after the tribunal. Until after they knew what was going to have to happen to Ethan and Ruby. Chances were this would all blow over, but he couldn't have Claire making a stink and tangling the web of problems further while he was trying to unravel it. No way was that girl staying quiet. She was hellfire and brimstone.

He tucked her phone into his jacket pocket as he made his way down the dock. He'd let her keep her purse, after making sure she didn't have a weapon in there. She was the sort of girl who would pack, an impressive and terrifying thought. He wasn't convinced a pistol-toting Claire would make the world a safer place. His first impressions of her said she was a shoot first, ask questions later sort of girl.

Not that he hadn't had a bit of experience on that front himself. He certainly hadn't planned on bringing her back to the reservation. She was so damned uncooperative. He'd had no choice.

The look on her face when she realized Ruby wasn't on the boat was one of rage mixed with betrayal. He wasn't going to lie. He felt a little bad about tricking her.

She didn't realize just how lucky she was to be at his place instead of the reservation lockup.

He checked her phone again. It was ten until six. The committee meeting was about to start. He had hoped to return in time to see Ethan again, but the trip to Seattle and back had eaten up most of the day. The meeting could go all night. If only Ethan had his damned phone, he could at least have called him. But Ethan didn't have a landline, and Jacob didn't have time to drive out to his place until morning if they didn't end up crossing paths later. In the forest.

Feeling its pull, he looked up at the tinge of moon glowing behind the stormy sky. They both needed to run.

Jacob got back into his car and drove to city hall.

***

Claire was exhausted. She'd trashed the bastard's precious boat. Or at least the level she was locked into. She'd pried and kicked and beaten at the window and door with everything she could find. Also, she'd screamed her fool head off for the first half hour, ruining her voice. Not that there was anyone to talk to.

How long did he think he could hold her here? What if he planned to take her out to sea and kill her there? He could tie something heavy to her body and sink her to the bottom of the Sound. No one would ever know what happened to her.

Anxiety swirled around her stomach. She should have known better than to get into the car with him, but she'd been certain he'd lead her to Ruby. That hadn't worked out so well. What the hell had they stumbled into? Some sort of weird cult? A bunch of serial killers? Worse?

Yeah, she couldn't think of anything worse. At least she wasn't tied up. What a bonus. No telling how long he planned to hold her here before he came back. Claire's stomach growled despite her worry.

Good grief.

She hadn't seen any food during her pillage and plunder stint around the cabin. Claire flopped back onto the bed, arms spread wide, and considered her options. Obviously, she was going to have to wait. He'd come back for her eventually. At least there was a tiny bathroom, although the thought of peeing right on his precious floor had occurred to her. But then she'd be the only one forced to suffer with it. She'd use the provided accommodations. She had a better plan.

Claire reached into her coat pocket. The asshole had searched her purse but not her body. His bad. She pulled the can of bear spray from her pocket and gripped it tightly. When Mr. Chandler returned, she'd have a surprise for him.

***

Jacob did not like the direction the meeting had taken. His crew was in position at Ethan's house, waiting for the thief to show. As soon as he did—and Jacob was certain he would—the cleaner crew would bring him out into the woods and have a come-to-the-Great-Spirit meeting with him. That tactic worked most of the time. Of course, nothing had gone his way so far today. He tried not to ponder on that fact too much as the council argued about Ethan's potential punishments. Poor guy hadn't even had a trial yet and his peers were ready to hang him out to dry.

Sure, he understood the sensitive nature of what they were protecting, but there would come a time—and maybe it was now—when the truth would come out. The Lummi and nearly every Native nation across the world had helped keep the secrets of the Sasquatch since the beginning of creation. The Nations revered the Sasquatch. For the most part, the Sasquatch lived up to their expectations. Only occasionally did one lose his humanity so completely as to cause irreparable damage and have to be put down.

This certainly wasn't the case with Ethan. No one had been hurt. Only Ethan's own reputation and identity were at stake. It was the witnesses, immediate and tangential, who were the bigger problem. But from the way the council was talking, they were ready to force Ethan's mate match for his transgression. They couldn't risk an excommunication because that would expose him and the clan further. But if they forced him to marry a clanswoman, he'd be bound to them and their way of life. And if he'd refused? Tried to run? The clan's trackers would hunt him until the end of his days. Euthanasia or commit to the clan were the two options presented for Ethan. So much for innocent before proven guilty.

This was Squatch justice at its worst, and Ethan would never stand for it.

"You haven't talked to Ethan yet, let alone his"—Jacob hesitated—"girlfriend." That was maybe pushing it. He knew how the Squatch half of the council would feel about Ethan having a normal for a girlfriend. Especially Joseph.

"I plan to talk with the girl myself," Joseph said. "First thing in the morning. Ethan can't continue in this manner. Our race will not survive unless each member carries it forward. Mating outside our race is the worst sort of treason."

Jacob interjected, "I think that thinking is a little old school, Joseph. I'm not saying I want to be the one to responsible for the extinction of Sasquatches, but you can't make a man or woman love someone they don't."

Joseph's face reddened, and the veins in his neck bulged. "The tribunal will decide that. We'll interview them both. Separately. Then present the case to be voted on by the tribe and clan. This affects us all. The vote will be final."

"And who decides the punishments, if any?" Jacob asked, looking pointedly at each of the other five council members.

The council members grew restless, avoiding eye contact with him.

"You do realize times are changing, whether you want them to or not. It's only a matter of time before we can't *clean up* a sighting. Consider as you run tonight," Jacob addressed Joseph and the other Squatch council representatives, "this may be that time."

"Not on my watch," Joseph said. "I'll see you in the woods."

Jacob left the council meeting feeling no more confident about its outcome than when he'd arrived. Even less so, considering he hadn't mentioned Ruby's roommate currently resided on his boat. It was nearly ten when he pulled up to the dock with three frozen burritos from the convenience store. They wouldn't be great, but his options were limited. He needed to drop off the food for Claire and get to the woods. A good run would clear his mind and tamp down his beast side, for a while anyway. Tomorrow would be a long day. He'd be lucky to get an hour or two of sleep in the morning before he had to collect Ethan and Ruby and sit in on the interviews.

He'd do what he could for Ethan. This vote could split the clan in two. There was more division than Joseph wanted to admit. Ethan wasn't the only one ready to abandon his Sasquatch heritage. There had been rumblings for years. Modern technology had made it damn near impossible to stay hidden and protect their families, even with the Lummi's help. He was certain other clans across the nation and the world faced the same issues.

His men at Ethan's house already had the thief in custody and were on their way back with him, their prisoner hogtied and stuffed in a trunk. Dude had shown up like Jacob had expected him to. He almost felt sorry for the bastard. He was in for a hell of a night. God, sometimes these guys were too easy.

And, other times, they were like Ruby…and Claire.

Jacob stepped onto the deck and paused at the door, key in hand, steeling himself for the wrath he was sure to find waiting for him on the other side. He pressed his ear to the door to see if he could discern what she might be up to. Silence.

Why did her silence send his insides stirring?

He slid the bolt to the left and turned the knob then pushed the door inward. The lights were out. Without his Squatch eyes, his night vision was only slightly better than any other humans. He squinted, trying to make out where she might be as he slid his free hand along the wall, searching for the switch.

"Claire? Are you sleeping? I brought you some dinner. Well, not really much of a—" Jacob flipped on the light long enough to see a bright-pink canister in front of his face. Then…pain. Pepper spray filled his eyes and nose before he realized what was happening. He dropped the burritos and his keys, clawing at his face. *Pain!* He knew he shouldn't rub at his eyes, that the action would only spread the peppery goo around more, but he couldn't help himself. His eyes wept.

He heard Claire scuffling along the floor beside him.

"Claire? Claire? Don't go!"

She pushed him hard, and he flailed about, trying to catch her, but it was too late. He tried to force his eyes open, but they refused to cooperate. He heard the door slam behind him then the pounding of her feet across the boat deck and into the night.

Goddamn it!

He felt his way to the bathroom and turned on the bathtub faucet. Bending over the side of the tub, he pushed his face into the stream and held it there, flushing his eyes with the cool water.

Shit! Shit! Shit!

No telling where she was by now. Did she pick up his keys? She knew what he drove. If she found his car, she'd go straight to the police. He had to get out there after her. Now!

He didn't have time to waste with his face under the faucet, but he forced himself to calm the hell down and endure it. A little more time spent under there, would mean a quicker recovery. He was a doctor, after all. There was a reason doctors were the worst patients. Telling someone what to do and experiencing it yourself were two different things.

Where the hell did she get that bear spray? He didn't own any. She had to have brought it herself. He'd checked her purse.

God, why hadn't he patted her down?

He didn't have time for this nonsense. Between the sting his men were working at Ethan's house, the tribunal tomorrow, his need to run, and now this? He couldn't do it all.

Shit.

Jacob pulled back from the stream and let the water drip from his soaked head and face. A few seconds later, he took a few tentative blinks, clearing the water from his lashes. His eyes burned, but it was tolerable. The bathroom blurred before him. He reached for a towel from above his head and patted carefully at his eyes and face.

When he shifted, the pain would go away. But how much longer before he could do that? Ethan was probably already in the forest, as were most of the clan. Jacob walked into the bedroom and spied his keys on the floor, exactly where he'd dropped them earlier.

Thank God for small favors.

That meant she was on foot, at least. And he had her scent. He could track her. But he could track her better in his Sasquatch form. Ironic the one thing he was trying hardest to avoid might be the only way to keep her out of further trouble.

Jacob shut the cabin door behind him as he walked out onto the deck. His vision was still a little blurry, and he couldn't see her anywhere. Not that he'd expected to, really. She was probably hiding. He inhaled deeply, searching for her scent. She'd run toward the woods. If the rain held off, he'd find her. He doubted she'd go too far in the dark.

He shifted on the deck of his boat and raced down the dock to the edge of the forest. For her own safety, he prayed he found her first.

Chapter Twelve

Faraday smoked in his car to calm his nerves as he kept a safe distance from the BFD van, which in turn followed the thief who was currently stuffed into the trunk of a car on the way to God only knew where. All he knew for sure was they were heading north out of Seattle along I-5. He prayed it wasn't a wild-goose chase. His gut told him it wasn't.

Earlier in the evening, he'd been staking out Lane's home, while Garret and his crew waited near the ferry lot, in case anyone showed. Too big a crowd would have drawn attention. Faraday was used to making himself inconspicuous. Besides, Lane's dumpsters had practically become his second home of late.

When the big black sedan arrived, Faraday had clicked off shots sans flash. Likely none would be usable, but habit forced him to comply. The garage bay door rose, and three men exited the vehicle then disappeared into the house. The driver drove away. Something was up. Lane was nowhere to be seen, but no lights came on inside after the men entered, and the house was silent as a tomb. The men were waiting for someone, and Faraday could hardly wait to see who it was.

An hour later, the thief had slunk through the wooded lot on the home's north side. Faraday held his position, praying he wouldn't be spotted. The thief made his way around the perimeter, checking windows for signs of activity. Finding none, the man made his move and broke out a small bathroom window on the back side then hauled himself through it and into the home.

Faraday envied his tenacity. If he hadn't watched the cadre of black-ops guys file into the home, he would have been tempted to follow. Instead, he waited to see what happened. A flash of light caught his attention, and he edged forward. Beams of light darted around the interior of the living area then landed on a body lying on the floor. Taser leads linked back to one of the men in black's gun. The thief was down. The other men hustled to gather the fallen man and carried him through the house and out of Faraday's line of sight. Darkness engulfed the interior once again. Faraday hustled quietly to the edge of the home, back to his original position seconds before the sedan returned and disappeared into the garage bay. The door went down. Faraday's heart pounded. There'd been no gunshots. He didn't think the man was dead. What were they going to do with him?

Several minutes later, the garage door went back up and the sedan backed out. He counted four men in the interior of the car, the driver and the three who'd entered the home, before the door closed and plunged them into darkness again. Where was the thief?

The car K-turned and headed down the street. As soon as the red taillights became pinpricks of light,

Faraday sprinted to his car, dialing his phone as he ran.

"Garrett, the black sedan. Don't lose it. Follow it. It's not Lane, but I have a pretty good idea they'll lead us to him. Don't let them out of your sight!"

Faraday had started his car and raced to make the last ferry off the island.

He flicked his cigarette out the cracked window then reached for another from a new pack. Filled with nicotine and adrenalin, he was pretty sure he could do this all night long if he had to.

***

The pull of the moon woke Ethan. A thin beam of moonlight broke through the storm clouds and pierced the window above his bed. Ruby stirred beside him but didn't wake. He didn't want to leave the warmth of his bed or Ruby's soft body. One biological need had been quenched for now. His other needs wouldn't be denied or satiated as easily. The sooner he shifted and ran, the sooner he could return to her.

They'd spent the rest of the evening talking in bed. There was no way to cover everything in such a short amount of time. They each had more than a quarter century of history to discuss. He prayed it would be enough to pacify the tribunal and convince them Ruby wouldn't expose their secret. The smallest flicker of hope sparked in his chest.

He was very curious how the council meeting had gone and hoped he'd find Jacob in the woods later. Conversation was primitive when they were in Squatch mode and mostly limited to grunts and whistles. Long distance communication consisted of tree knocks and was used as a primitive sort of Sasquatch Morse-like code. Once they shifted back, they could catch up in more detail.

Everything changed when he shifted. It was a special kind of magic he could never explain to someone who hadn't experienced it. Resisting it was painful beyond words. He'd seen himself more times than he cared to remember, his monstrous face reflected in the water as he drank from streams and pools.

He knew how fearsome his Sasquatch form was, which was why it still amazed him Ruby was in his bed beside him. After what she'd seen? He'd never really fleshed out his live-life-as-a-normal plan. He'd only really expected to try to date a bit. But now? After being with Ruby?

Ethan wanted a normal life more than ever.

No matter what it took, he'd see to it that she was safe and protected from the clan if things didn't go their way with the vote. Hell, he hoped it didn't actually come to a vote. The council could decide to forgo a vote, if they deemed Ruby harmless. He'd take whatever punishment they meted out for him as long as she was free to resume her life. He'd played out dozens of potential scenarios in his mind while he lay next to her, trying to decide on the best course of action. Maybe the secret-baby plan wasn't the best after all. God, he didn't know what to do. They would use that as their very last option. Maybe the shifted run tonight would clear his mind.

He eased out of bed, careful not to wake Ruby, and made his way to the door. No need for clothes. He'd be covered in hair seconds after he shut the door and then mostly protected from the elements. The rain would still be cold but tolerable. His hair would insulate him. Not the most enjoyable time of the year, but certainly better than summer. Most Sasquatch sightings were in the summer, when hikers made it into the back country. No one would be out wandering in this weather. Even if they were, everyone on the reservation was a friend. He was safe to let his wild side roam free for a few hours.

Ethan clicked the door shut behind him, shivering naked in the rain for a moment as he tried to relax into the change. Gooseflesh raised along his arms and legs first. Not unusual, all things considered, but then the hair sprouted like a thousand tiny pinpricks. He watched his hands tremble and grow twice their size. The long bones of his legs and arms elongated, and his back hunched in agony as his vertebrae expanded. His nails blackened into bear-like claws, and his face contorted and morphed. Ethan dropped to his knees as the final surge overtook him, extinguishing his visible humanity. His most primal instincts surged through him, and he ran, screaming into the dark forest, listening for the call of his kindred.

***

Ruby woke to an inhuman scream somewhere outside the cabin. Then a reply sounded in the distance. She sat up, searching for Ethan. *Gone*. Pulling the covers tighter, she curled into a ball, clutching her knees to her chest, and listened as more howls and whistles joined the first. He'd said he would have to leave and explained to her what it would entail, but hearing them outside her window in the darkness was unnerving. She'd grown up on the plains with plenty of midnight serenades from packs of coyotes, but this…was something different. Foreign. Unnatural.

She shuddered.

Ethan was one of them. Inhuman. No, more than human, because he was also kind and loving. Whatever his most primal nature, he was also one of the best men she'd ever met. Regardless of their differences, she was drawn to him in a way she couldn't explain. She should be getting into his car and driving the hell out of here. Instead, she burrowed deeper into the warmth of their bed and prayed he'd be home soon.

Home?

Everything had happened so quickly. And they were about to embark on a ridiculous lie that would bind them together further. At least until the tribe was satisfied with her compliance. She didn't want Ethan to be punished for something he couldn't control and swore she'd do whatever it took to protect him.

God, what would Claire think of all of this? She'd never be able to explain it to her. Not that she could anyway. No way would she drag her in further than she already had. Ruby hoped Claire didn't do anything stupid and heroic while she was gone. First thing in the morning, she needed to get to a phone and assure Claire she was okay.

Ruby listened hard. The Sasquatches had moved on. Deeper into the forest somewhere. Ruby relaxed again. The rain had stopped so the only sound was the still-crackling fire. The last log Ethan had put into the stove had been huge. An all-night log, he'd said. The hypnotizing sound lulled her back to sleep as she hugged Ethan's pillow snug to her body.

***

Ethan joined the clan sometime near dawn. There were more Sasquatches gathered in the forest this time than usual. The others circled around something, but he couldn't make it out. They were excited though, grunting and whistling. He recognized Elizabeth and for once was thankful to be in his animal form and not have to make up excuses for his long absence. She didn't seem to notice him.

As he got closer, he saw one of the women was poking at something with a stick…no…someone—curled up on the ground. A man.

Ethan inhaled sharply, trying to catch the scent and knew immediately who it was. It was the thief. Holy shit, they'd found him, and now he was getting some Sasquatch justice.

The man wailed, begging for his life. Colton Daniels kicked at him with his big meaty foot, pitching him forward and into the cold mud, which sent the man into a fresh torrent of pleas and tears. None of them could communicate in human language with the man while they were shifted. Not that they'd want to. This was all about ensuring no one would ever believe his story. Especially one of being bullied by a gang of Sasquatches. The guy could tell all the bullshit he wanted after tonight. Truth really was stranger than fiction, and this guy was getting a full measure of it.

Ethan almost felt sorry for the poor bastard. Almost.

Finally, Edward Collins and Jason Smallwood hefted the quivering excuse for a thief up from the ground and half dragged him toward the road, making sure he'd find his way there. Two Lummi men awaited in a car a half mile away to happen by in a few minutes to pick up the wandering stranger. It wouldn't do to let the man die of exposure out here. That would only bring more focus to his story. The two men would drive him back to Seattle and deposit him at his home. Ethan felt confident there wouldn't be any more official statements. From the look of the guy, he wouldn't be speaking any complete sentences for a while, let alone telling the media any more Sasquatch stories.

Their work here was done.

The fun over, a couple of the males sparred a bit more and carried on while others paired up and disappeared into the night again. They didn't have much longer before they'd have to shift back and be home. Daytime sightings weren't much of a worry on the reservation, but there was no reason to be careless. Ethan began making his way back toward the cabin.

The storm having passed, the sky began to lighten in the east. Ethan picked up his pace.

More than halfway home, a non-Sasquatch scream startled him. It was a long way off, toward the dock, maybe two miles or more, and in the opposite direction of home. Ruby? Could it be her? How?

The screams continued. Fear coursed through him, and he raced toward the sound. Had the others heard, or were they already home? What if one of them reached her first?

Ethan tore through the brush, the branches shredding his arms and legs and tearing out great tufts of hair. His heart pounded and a terrible anger built inside his chest. If one of them had hurt Ruby, there wouldn't be a tribunal, there would be a funeral. The screams grew louder and two scents reached him before he saw them. Jacob and someone else. Someone unfamiliar.

He broke into a small clearing and saw Jacob in his Sasquatch form carrying a struggling woman under his arm like King Kong with Fay Wray. It would have been laughable if he'd seen it in a movie and not a few hundred feet in front of him, in his real life.

What. The. Hell?

Ethan roared, and Jacob turned, his face fierce, ready to challenge him. Ethan held his hands up in a submissive gesture, reassuring his friend he meant no harm. He vocalized a series of soft huffs, letting Jacob know who he was. The woman bit down on Jacob's arm, and a roar of pain and frustration echoed across the clearing. Ethan motioned for Jacob to follow him back to the cabin. Jacob hesitated, and the woman nearly squirmed away. He tightened his grip and stomped toward Ethan, eyes glowing red. He was pissed. They made their way home in silence, except for the woman who cursed and fought the entire way.

Ethan had no idea what was going on, or why Jacob had captured a woman and exposed himself as a Sasquatch, but the tribunal may have become a whole lot more crowded.

God, Ethan couldn't wait to shift back. It felt like everything had gone sideways. His time with Ruby seemed like a dream. And now this mess with Jacob?

The sky cleared a bit, and moonlight brightened the night enough for Ethan to see smoke curling from his tiny cabin. Surely Jacob didn't intend to let his captive see him shift? Or had she already, and that's why he'd taken her? Ethan had ten thousand questions for his friend. Now he knew what Jacob must have felt like coming to save his ass last night. Was that only last night?

The woman continued to struggle, not giving up one bit. Jacob's arm bled from her repeated bites. When they finally got to his door, Jacob huffed and whistled. Ethan wasn't sure, but he trusted his friend and agreed then turned the knob and opened the door for him. Jacob tossed the woman into the room and slammed the door, trapping her in the cabin…with Ruby.

***

Ruby startled awake. "Ethan?" she asked, trying to make out what or who had come into the cabin.

The figure froze. Ruby dragged the blanket from the bed and pulled it around her naked body.

"Ruby?" a woman said.

Ruby blinked, trying to reconcile the voice with the mystery person in their cabin. "Claire?"

"Oh God, Ruby! I thought that monster was going to kill me. Ruby, we have to block the door. Hurry, help me!"

Claire grabbed the wooden arm of the futon and started dragging it across the hardwood floor to barricade the door. She had it pulled halfway across the small room before Ruby reached her.

"Claire! It's okay. You're safe here." Ruby reached to grab the other arm of the futon and slow her progress.

"Ruby, you didn't see it! It was hairy and it smelled like…like…a wet bear that had rolled in garbage. It was awful! And claws! Teeth! There were two of them, Ruby. I don't know why they let me go, but they are not getting into this cabin. Help me!"

Claire gave a great tug and slid the futon a foot more. Ruby flopped down on the couch to further impede her progress.

"Ruby! What are you doing? What's wrong with you? Out there. Just outside the door is a…a…"

"Sasquatch?" Ruby asked softly.

Claire stilled. "Yes," she whispered.

Ruby reached across the couch and put her hand over Claire's. "It's okay. He's…a friend. The Sasquatch is…Ethan."

Claire stared at her with big saucer-shaped eyes for a full ten seconds then re-launched into survival mode.

"You've been drugged. It's okay. I've got this. Just get off the couch, Ruby, and go grab that skillet over there. We can use it for a weapon."

In a surge of superhuman strength, Claire lifted the futon, dragging the couch and Ruby the remaining few feet in front of the door. "Ruby! Skillet! Move!"

"How did you get here, Claire? I mean, I don't even know exactly where I am. How did you find me?"

"Some guy kidnapped me. Said he was a friend of Ethan and yours. I blackmailed him to bring me to you. Then he locked me on a fucking boat instead. When he came back, I pepper sprayed him and ran into the woods. Then that…thing grabbed me."

"It wasn't a thing. You know what it was, Claire. They aren't the monsters you think they are. Or…at least Ethan isn't."

"Okay, Ruby, look at me." Claire grabbed her by the shoulders; her blanket slid a bit. "Wait, you're naked?"

"Well, yeah."

"Why are you naked? What have they been doing to you?"

"Nothing! I mean, not yet anyway. Ethan and I—"

"You have Stockholm Syndrome. You're not thinking straight. Get your clothes on. I'll look for some weapons. We're getting out of here." Claire turned her by the shoulders and gave her a little shove toward the bathroom then began rummaging through drawers.

Ruby did put her clothes back on, but she had no intention of leaving without Ethan. What was taking him so long? The cabin grew lighter as the sun began to rise. Ruby's stomach did a little flip-flop. On the one hand, she was happy to see Claire! On the other, now her friend was as deeply involved as she was. At least Ruby'd had a couple of days to adjust to the whole Sasquatch-is-real thing. Claire was clearly going to take a bit more convincing. Nearly dressed, she was pulling up her tights when the front door pushed open a bit, scraping the futon across the floor.

"Ruby?" Ethan asked, tentatively.

"Ethan! Let me move the couch." Ruby raced across the cabin.

"No!" Claire yelled, wielding a knife from the kitchenette.

"Stop it. Right now." Ruby put her body between the futon and the door.

"Um, Ruby. I need my clothes. And bring another change, too, please…for Jacob," Ethan said through the opening.

"You'll do no such thing, Ruby. Jacob is who kidnapped me! Leave them out there with the monsters."

"Just a minute, Ethan." Ruby gathered his clothes then went to his armoire for another change.

Claire stood between her and the door. "You are not going out there, Ruby."

"I won't, but I am giving Ethan clothes. And then we are going to let them in so we can figure this out."

Ruby eased past her, shoving the clothing through the gap.

"Thanks," Ethan said, giving her hand a little squeeze.

"You're welcome."

"Oh. My. God. You have been completely brainwashed. Seriously, I saw a documentary about this."

"I doubt anyone has made a documentary about this," Ruby said. "Help me move this futon back."

"I'm surprised they haven't already dyed your hair and marked you with their cult tattoos or something," Claire said.

Ruby pushed at the futon, inching it away from the door. "It's not like that. Ethan is trying to protect me. To protect us all."

"Seems to me if they hadn't kidnapped us both, we wouldn't need protecting."

The door pushed open slowly. "We're coming in," Ethan said.

He walked through first, steering clear of Claire. Ruby ran to him, wrapping her arms around his neck. Ethan leaned down and kissed her, keeping one eye on Claire.

"Are you all right?" Ruby asked, stroking his smooth, hairless face in amazement.

"Better." Ethan curled his arm around Ruby's waist and faced Claire. "So this must be your roommate?"

"Yes. Claire meet Ethan. My *Daveslist* date. The one you set me up with. Remember that?"

"You don't look old enough to have written all those books," Claire said, instantly reminding Ruby of their increasingly tangled web.

Jacob walked in next. Claire's eyes flashed with anger. She gripped the knife hard enough to turn her knuckles white. Jacob's eyes were bloodshot and weepy, like he'd been crying, which made no sense at all to Ruby. What was wrong with him?

"You look like shit," Claire said pointedly to Jacob.

"You get sprayed in the face with bear spray and see how you feel," he replied.

"Bear spray? Claire, you didn't."

"Oh yeah I did. I would have gotten away, too, if not for that…thing."

Ethan pulled Ruby in tight against his body, his arms strong and warm around her, reminding her of their night together.

"She's not going to believe it until she sees it herself, Jacob. You're going to have to show her," Ethan said.

"This is the most fucked-up night of my life," Jacob said.

"Show me what?" Claire asked.

Jacob sighed then took off his shirt and unbuttoned his pants.

Claire blanched. "Listen, I don't know what sort of messed-up, nightmare, voodoo craziness you all have going on out here, but—Mother of God, what's happening to him?"

Jacob began to shift.

Claire fainted.

***

Ethan scooped up Ruby's friend Claire and deposited her on the futon. This had gone wrong, wrong, wrong. The last thing they needed was yet another eye witness to their clan secret, but after Jacob had told him outside the cabin what had happened, it seemed like the only choice. Claire wasn't going to let it go and wait for Ruby to come home.

"I can't believe she passed out." Ruby dabbed at Claire's face with a cold rag.

"It's a lot to take in. Adrenalin coursing through her. It can cause a huge crash," Jacob said, pacing the short distance from couch to door. He was going to wear a rut in the floor. "And she hasn't eaten."

"What time are the tribunal interviews?" Ethan asked.

"Two hours," Jacob said. "I should be there now."

"No one else knows Claire is here, Jacob," Ethan said. "We can keep her out of this. Not complicate the situation further."

"You think she's going to let that happen? Have you met her?"

"I can talk to her," Ruby said. "I can convince her."

Jacob shot Ethan an exasperated look. "I have to go."

"Take my car," Ethan said. "Send Henry to pick Ruby and me up. We'll take care of the Claire problem."

Jacob looked skeptical. "I don't think anyone can take care of that problem."

***

Claire began to stir. "Claire? Claire. Wake up. We don't have much time."

"What the…" Claire scrambled upright and to the end of the futon, looking around wildly as she gathered her senses. Her gaze landed on Ethan, and she froze.

"No, you're safe. Ethan is our friend."

"Where's the other one? I want to go home. Right now. You're coming with me, Ruby." Claire rose from the futon and headed toward the door.

Ethan stepped into her path, looming over her. "You can go home. But not yet."

"Move, hairball." Claire rose up to her full five foot two and faced off against him. It would have been comical if so much wasn't riding on her cooperation.

"Claire, we have an hour to explain and then you have to make a decision that could seal all of our fates. Shut up and sit down." Ruby rested her hand on Claire's tense shoulder. "Please."

Claire took a step back from Ethan, her eyes never leaving his as she eased back to the futon. Her lips pressed into a thin line, as she struggled against her nature to maintain control. She leaned forward, her hands folded together in her lap, over her knees. "Start talking."

Ruby did. She laid out the whole story from when Claire dropped her off at the Annex until now. Ethan chimed in on occasion, but his contributions seemed only to irritate Claire further. Eventually, he worked at maintaining the fire in the wood stove while Ruby talked. Claire watched him like a hawk until the story was told.

Claire sat back and tilted her face toward the ceiling. Her eyes closed as she processed. "Let me get this straight. Ethan is a Sasquatch shifter. Jacob is a

Sasquatch shifter. There is an entire clan of Sasquatch shifters, right here, on the Lummi Reservation, in my home state, and there always has been. You, my naive Midwestern roommate, are in love with one of them, who also happens to be a world famous author who's been hiding behind a secret identity for the past decade. And now, because you know his secrets, you're about to be judged by a Lummi/Sasquatch council to determine whether or not you can be trusted with the secret or if you'll be 'contained' somehow? Does that sum it up?"

Ethan stopped fiddling with the stove, and Ruby caught his gaze.

"Yes. That's the whole thing," she said.

"And if the clan decides you aren't worthy of this secret?" Claire asked.

"They'll decide a punishment…and carry it out," Ethan said.

"What kind of punishment are we talking here, Ethan? Be specific."

"Most likely, they'll make her an unreliable witness by ruining her reputation, her career, discrediting her in every way they can. She'll be a laughingstock. Without physical evidence, the word of a civilian isn't worth all that much. This time, there is some video evidence, but I can't be identified except by Ruby…and now you."

"So if I stay quiet, I can stay out of this tribunal thing?"

"Yes."

"And this is what you want, Ruby?"

Ruby reached for Ethan's hand. "Yes."

"Okay."

Ethan looked at Ruby with surprise. "Okay?"

"Okay to Ruby, not to you. I couldn't care less what happens to you, but if my staying here and being quiet for a few hours will help Ruby, I'll do it."

Ruby squeezed his hand then let go, walking over to sit beside her friend. She curled an arm around Claire's shoulders and hugged her. "Thank you. It's all going to be fine. I promise."

Claire's icy glare lasered onto Ethan. "It had better be."

Chapter Thirteen

Faraday was torn. The men from the black sedan had carried the man, still unconscious as far as he could tell, into the thick woods of the Lummi reservation and returned without him, leaving him to assume the man was now most likely dead and buried. He'd hidden his own car more than a mile past their drop-off point and slunk through the edge of the forest until he had a clear view. Thank God for the full moon. Garrett and his team had continued on. No way to hide that damned emblazoned van. For Garrett, that was the point though. He didn't want to be in the shadows. He'd continued around the peninsula's loop road, waiting for Faraday's report, which so far consisted of nothing Sasquatch worthy.

Some sort of craziness was going down, however. Faraday couldn't risk a camera flash giving away his location, so he sat and watched and waited. And waited, deciding he'd venture into the woods and search for the man's grave after they left. Except they didn't really leave. They backed down the road and parked, just shy of discovering his own car's hiding place, thank God, and waited themselves.

Faraday was forced to hang tight in the biting cold. He hunkered down and waited some more.

When the man finally wandered drunkenly out of the woods on his own, a different vehicle drove past and stopped to pick him up. The thief willingly got into the car, and Faraday raced through the brambles to his vehicle to follow them.

***

The "interviews" lasted all day, with Ethan being interrogated in one room, and Ruby a floor above him in Joseph's office with Jacob. It was excruciating. Ethan was exhausted and worried. They'd asked him much more intrusive questions concerning Ruby than he'd anticipated. He'd answered as vaguely as possible, leaving lots of wiggle room for massaging Ruby's answers into a believable story later. They hadn't had enough time together, and the time they had spent together, they'd been…well…*together*. Not that he regretted that. Only the timing.

He hadn't played the secret-baby card. He couldn't. He prayed Ruby hadn't either. If their stories didn't match…

Finally dismissed, Ethan made his way upstairs and eavesdropped outside Joseph's office door, listening to the rise and fall of voices inside. He heard boots stomping hurriedly up the old wooden stairs from below and turned to look. Elizabeth made her way toward Joseph's office like she was on a mission. She started when she looked up to see Ethan sitting in a chair outside.

"Oh, hi, Ethan," she said, sliding her hand into her jeans' pocket.

"Hello, Elizabeth."

"How's it going? In there?"

"You know about all this?" Ethan asked, rising from his chair and stepping toward her.

"Only a bit. Dad just told me to come down here. Make sure I was in attendance." She blushed. "I'm sorry. About everything."

Ethan shrugged. "It's no one's fault but my own."

"I know this isn't what you want." She hesitated. "That I'm not what you want."

"Elizabeth, I'm sorry about the way I left. It's not you. It's me. You're amazing."

"Right."

"You are. I just don't feel that way about you."

"I know. It's fine. Dad was more upset about it than I was. Really. I get it. If I could change it—"

The door swung open, and Jacob held it for Ruby to exit. Her face was pale as her eyes darted from Elizabeth to him, clearly wondering what was going on. Ethan approached her and wrapped an arm around her waist, leaning in to brush a kiss against her cheek then whispered in her ear, "You okay?"

Ruby nodded slightly, but she wasn't selling it.

"Elizabeth?" Joseph called from behind his desk.

"Yes, Daddy," Elizabeth said.

"Come on in. Jacob?"

"Yeah?"

"Tomorrow."

Jacob pinched the bridge of his nose. "Yep."

"Good luck," Elizabeth said as she headed into Joseph's office.

"You, too," Jacob said.

The door closed behind her, and Jacob grabbed Ethan's arm, leading him away quickly toward the stairs.

"How did—" Ethan started.

"Not yet. Let's get to the car first."

Ethan pulled her along behind him as they followed Jacob to the surprising darkness of the parking lot. They'd arrived in the daylight and lost the entire day. The cold wind bit his face. He opened the back door for Ruby then walked around to slide in beside her on the back passenger side, leaving Jacob to chauffeur them.

The doors shut, and Jacob slammed his head back against the headrest, his closed eyes reflected in the rearview mirror.

"What's up, Jacob? How did it go?"

Jacob shot a look in the mirror at Ruby. "She did great. Better than I'd expected, but it's not going to matter."

Ethan took Ruby's icy-cold hand into his, and a tear rolled down her face. "I don't understand. Why won't it matter?"

"Joe's taking this opportunity to push his match on you. To force you to marry Elizabeth and seal your bond with the clan. That's why Elizabeth was there. He's going to tell her next."

Rage boiled up from Ethan's gut and filled him. "He can't make me marry Elizabeth. I won't do it."

"He's got a compelling case, Ethan. The clan will vote to protect itself, not an outsider."

"So the tribunal vote is a farce? He's already made the decision? That's absolute bullshit. This is exactly why the clan will become extinct. Not cell phones and cameras, but tyrannical leadership like this. I won't do it. He can't make me."

"He threatened my family, Ethan," Ruby said, her voice small and quiet.

"How?" Ethan asked, looking at Jacob for the answer.

"Joe threatened to send the Horner clan over to pay them a visit."

"So that's what we've come to now? Mafia-style intimidation? Hell, his own daughter doesn't want this anymore."

Ethan was tired. Tired of living in fear. Tired of hiding what he was and tired of living a life full of lies. Ruby was the best thing to happen to him in…ever. There was no way he was going to leave her fate up to a handful of old men fearful of change.

A black van pulled into the city hall lot and parked several rows over. "Shit," Jacob said, turning off his engine.

"What is it?" Ruby asked.

Ethan leaned across her for a better look. *BFD "We're Squatching You"* was emblazoned on the side panel.

"What's BFD?" Ruby asked.

"*Bigfoot Field Department*," Ethan said.

"You mean like the television show?" Ruby squeaked.

"Exactly like the show. How the hell did they end up here?" Ethan asked.

Jacob shook his head then slammed it back into the headrest. "They must have followed me back from Claire's place or something. Either that or the thief's re-education didn't take. What the fuck are we going to do now?"

Several long moments of silence filled the car.

"Maybe it's time we come clean," Ethan said.

"We?" Jacob asked, his gaze snapping up to the mirror.

"Me. Someone needs to be the spokesperson. With my high profile and standing as Robin Woodring, it might be the best chance for acceptance. Maybe the only way to truly be free is to…be free."

"What are you saying?" Jacob asked.

"How do we beat an adversary, Jacob? You told me on the boat."

"Find the weakness and use it against them." Jacob turned and leaned back between the seats so he could see them both, his eyes narrowed. "What do you have in mind?"

Ethan smiled. "Are you up for a plot twist?"

Jacob sucked in a long breath then exhaled. "Let's give 'em what they came for."

***

Two BFD hunters piled out of the van; one gripped a handheld camera and fumbled with sound equipment. Ethan, Ruby, and Jacob exited the car. Ethan glanced around the lot, nervous he couldn't complete the task before the council intervened. He needed time. Time to give them exactly what they sought and break this mess wide open. A secret only held power if it remained a secret for others to expose. If Sasquatch shifters were outed to the light of day, the power returned to Ethan. He controlled the story.

He would limit the exposure to himself. One Sasquatch would be enough to keep them busy for a good long time. Then, later, after the dust settled, maybe others could and would come out. If the world wanted to believe in one Bigfoot, Ethan was ready to be that guy.

The council was bound to vote against him, and there was no way in hell he was marrying Elizabeth. If they wanted some justice, let it start now.

He'd not broken any government laws, only the clan's laws. And while there'd be great curiosity, he wouldn't allow himself to be prodded and poked. Security would be an issue, but then, as soon as his author identity was exposed, which was inevitable, he'd have needed to upgrade that anyway.

He'd tried to convince Ruby to stay in the car, but she'd refused. His chest tightened as they walked across the lot. He took Ruby's hand in his and leaned in. "You can bail at any time. You don't have to be a part of this. When we get back to the cabin, take Jacob's car and drive home. The clan won't have any reason to follow you after this breaks."

Ruby halted, pulling him to a stop as well. "No. I want to do this. I want…to be with you."

Relief coursed through him and lit the tiniest flames of hope deep inside him. This was by far the craziest thing he'd ever done. Crazier even than going on a blind date with a normal. He shot a look to Jacob, who shrugged at him, eyebrows raised in question.

"You sure?" Jacob asked, as the BFD hunters turned their way.

"Yeah," Ethan answered, and strode forward with his hand extended in greeting.

The middle-aged bearded man saw him first and smiled, reaching for Ethan's offered hand. "Howdy. Garret Decker, BFD Field Agent. We're looking for the tribe president...Joseph Ballew?"

"Ethan Lane. May I ask why you're looking for Joseph?"

"Well, I guess you can see our vans aren't too subtle." He chuckled. "There was a Bigfoot sighting in downtown Seattle recently, and the witness contacted us claiming he'd been kidnapped and brought out here to the reservation and…well…harassed."

"That sounds pretty unlikely," Ethan said. "What makes you think that could be true?"

"He had a handful of hair he'd pulled out of one of his abductors. Our cryptozoologist can't seem to identify it as any known creature."

"Still could have been fabricated," Jacob chimed in.

"Maybe. He also had sound recordings from his phone. He'd managed to turn it on in the trunk before he was dragged out and dropped along the woods. Not long after that, *they* came."

"And who would *they* be?" Jacob asked.

"The only *they* we care about. Sasquatches," Garret said.

"So you're here to do what, then?" Ethan asked, growing more and more nervous they would be discovered by the council. The BFD vans would have been spotted as soon as they ventured onto the reservation. The only reason Joseph wasn't already out here running them off was because he was currently embroiled with the council, sealing Ethan and Ruby's fate. Or so he thought.

"Find out the truth about Sasquatches. Prove they exist," Garret said.

"And then what?" Jacob asked.

"Break this story wide open so the world can finally know."

"And what if they aren't what you expect? What if they want to live their lives in peace?" Ethan asked.

Garret cocked his head to the side, studying Ethan. "The truth is out there. I'd like to see it."

Ethan allowed the shift to rise up from deep inside him and let his eyes flash red. "You're going to want to follow us."

Chapter Fourteen

Ethan rode in the passenger seat of the BFD van while Garrett drove. His skittish cameraman sat quietly on the panel van's floor behind him. Ethan's eye shift had had the desired effect. The BFD were interested. For all their reality show bravado on TV, they were suddenly very in and very out of their element. Garret gripped the steering wheel tightly as they made their way down the long driveway to the cabin. They'd managed to make it out of the parking lot before the council was alerted. Still, he knew they didn't have much time.

Joseph would bring the full force of the clan down upon them within the hour, if not sooner, as they began to piece together who had been in the parking lot and where they'd gone. The van came to a stop. Jacob's headlights shone in the side mirrors. Ethan exited the van and walked around to the front of the vehicle. The side doors opened and the crew bailed out, each one laden with equipment.

Garret joined him at the front of the van. "What is it you want to show us, Mr. Chandler? I have to tell you, I'm a little uncomfortable."

Ethan laughed. “How long have you been hunting Bigfoot, Mr. Decker?”

“Nearly twenty years,” Garret said.

“And what evidence have you discovered other than blurry videos and footprints?”

Garret smiled ruefully. “Nothing conclusive.”

“Yet you believe? You still hunt? Or is that all for the show?”

“I believe,” Garret said.

“Haven’t you wondered why there’s never been any irrefutable evidence like bones or fossils or, heck, a Sasquatch corpse?”

Garret shifted uncomfortably. “Of course.”

“What if Sasquatch can change forms. Sometimes a man and sometimes a Sasquatch?” Ethan asked.

“That’s not possible.”

“Oh? And why not? You believe in a mythical creature but not in supernatural magic of transmutation? That seems a bit shortsighted.”

“There’s no proof that could even happen. No eye witnesses. No video evidence.” Garrett looked around, suddenly visibly nervous but too curious to retreat.

“Can you live broadcast, Mr. Decker?” Ethan asked.

“We can, we need to run up the antenna and get set up.”

“Fire up those cameras. We’re about to make history.”

Ethan leaned in to Ruby and whispered in her ear. “Keep Claire occupied so Jacob can help me. Things are about to get crazy.”

Ruby turned and kissed his cheek. “Be careful.”

Ethan smiled as fear curdled in his gut. “Always.”

Ruby hurried to the doorway of the cabin where Claire stood, straining against Jacob’s firm hold on her as he tried to keep her out of the impending fray. Ethan's skin itched and tingled in anticipation of another shift so soon. They needed to hurry and get this all documented before the clan council arrived.

Jacob stepped up beside him. "You ready for this?"

"As ready as I'll ever be. You're going to want to get out of the camera view. No need dragging any more down than necessary," Ethan said sidestepping away from his friend.

"Bullshit. We do this together," Jacob said.

Ethan whipped around to face him. "No, Jacob. Don't do this."

"If you're going to come out, I am, too. You're a world renowned author. I'm a doctor. People know us. The government can't very well hide us away in a secret lab without repercussions."

"But the clan—" Ethan retorted.

"The clan can bite me. Change was coming whether they wanted it to or not. Time to herald in a new era."

Ethan swallowed hard then clapped a hand on Jacob's back. "Thanks."

"Yep. Let's get squatchy."

Garrett approached from the van, his cameraman in tow. Another crew member had jacked up the satellite antenna, ready for live transmission. "Sammy's ready when you are. Want to give me some idea of what you have in mind here?"

"I'm afraid you'll have to see it to believe it. Keep that camera recording. Probably ought to have your crew roll some cell footage, too. We're about to get real crowded. Best not to have all our eggs in one basket."

Garrett nodded to his crew and phones lit up like fireflies in the darkness. “When you’re ready, Mr. Lane. We’re recording and transmitting.”

Ethan heard the crunch of gravel as the first car skidded onto his long driveway. He closed his eyes and summoned the shift. He sensed Jacob doing the same next to him. Hair sprouted and grew coarse and long beneath his clothing as his muscle and bone succumbed to his natural inclination. Adrenalin flooded his transmuting body, pushing the fear he’d felt earlier away and filling him with righteousness. Escaping his destiny wasn’t the answer. Embracing his essence. This was the answer. Seconds later his clothing was in tatters and his body had been transformed to his full Sasquatch glory. The cameraman’s Sony shook in his hands, and he nearly dropped it before Garrett caught it and steadied it.

Ethan turned to see Jacob, also shifted, by his side. Jacob’s squatchy mouth curled into a menacing grin, baring sharp incisors. A soft chortle betrayed his visual menace, indicating to Ethan he was pleased, but the tone was lost on the spectators.

A gasp sounded from one of Garrett’s crew. Mouths gaped, and the only sound was the quickly approaching parade of vehicles.

“Did you get that, Sam? For the love of God, tell me you got that,” Garret said.

For effect, Ethan growled, and the stench of urine filled his nose. The cameraman’s bladder had released. Headlights illuminated their little gathering as cars skidded to a stop. Lummi and Sasquatch alike poured out of the caravan of vehicles, racing toward Ethan and Jacob.

Unless every recording device had failed, or the council planned a mass homicide, the Sasquatch were out of the shadows. No way the whammy could be applied to so many. Garrett was a high profile television host, for God's sake. There was no going back and no scrubbing a sighting this large and with this many witnesses.

Joseph approached and stood before Ethan, the top of his head barely coming to Ethan's squatchy elbow while the man was still in his human form. Unintimidated, Joseph lasered his hatred at Ethan.

"What have you done?" Joseph asked, vitriol dripping.

"Freed us," Ethan grunted.

The clicking of a camera caught his attention, and he saw Faraday, his Nikon pointed directly at the two of them. Somehow, he wasn't surprised. Ethan turned to the reporter and gave him exactly what he'd come for as he shifted back.

***

The chapel was packed. There'd never been this many people on a Sunday, let alone for a Lummi/Clan meeting. And Ethan couldn't remember when they'd had the last full-fledged tribunal. He wasn't thrilled to be the impetus for this emergency meeting, but here they were, an hour after his broadcast went live. The parking lot was filling up outside with news vans, Bigfoot fans, and spectators. The "outing" was unprecedented and completely unexpected. Ethan was prepared to face the consequences because the alternative for him and Ruby was worse. He'd brokered a tentative but exclusive deal with Garrett and Faraday. He prayed it would hold.

Ethan led Ruby down the aisle by the hand, feeling the weight of the three hundred some sets of eyes on them as they made their way to the front pew. Jacob sat at the council table on the small stage, next to Joseph. He was still a full council member. At least until this meeting was over. Elizabeth sat in the front row on the right side of the aisle, looking like she was about to throw up. She didn't make eye contact.

Ethan urged Ruby to sit next to Claire on the left side of the aisle in the front row, too. Claire was sedate and quiet for the first time since he'd met her.

Ruby's hand trembled in his. This would be okay. He'd make it okay.

They sat and waited.

The mumbling of the crowd behind them picked up, and Ethan's confidence began to wane. Maybe he and Ruby should have run after all that had happened. But, if they had, they'd never have been able to stop. There were clans everywhere. Every indigenous clan in the world supported and protected a Sasquatch clan. He knew he wasn't the only one who wanted change. He wasn't the only one who wanted to be free of this curse. It was time someone stood up and demanded a change. And, now, change would come, whether they wanted it to or not.

And with a growing horde of reporters and news teams from around the world waiting outside the chapel doors, there was no going back now. More would come. This was only the first wave. Still, the clan would have its justice. One way or another.

Joe hammered a wooden gavel on the long plastic table, and the crowd hushed. "Thank you all for coming. As co-president of the Lummi/Sasquatch council, and in light of recent publically documented transgressions, this tribunal has been convened to determine how to proceed."

Grumbles of discontent swept through the crowd.

Jacob rose behind the table. "As you have probably seen, the footage of Ethan and I shifting has been published on King5 and the Internet. There were many witnesses. This was intentional. Not accidental. Ethan's downtown shift originally exposed him, but, as time went on, it became apparent there would be no containing this incident. I chose to stand with Ethan. That doesn't mean any of the rest of you have to. Not now or ever. We are willing to shoulder the burden of this exposure because, in our hearts, we both want to be free of this curse. It's my belief others in this clan feel the same way. That's for you to decide as individuals, but no one has to decide anything today."

Ethan squeezed Ruby's hand and rose then walked the few steps to stand in front of the council tables. He shoved his hands down into his front jeans' pockets and rocked back onto his heels, facing the crowd. The council loomed on the stage behind and above him.

"The council and clan may now ask questions if they'd like," Jacob announced.

As expected, Joe spoke first. "How could you do this to us, Ethan? You are a traitor to our clan and our heritage."

Ethan tensed. His next answer would stir the hornet's nest. "I don't want to shift anymore. I want to be normal. I want to have a normal life."

The crowd erupted into pandemonium.

"So you admit to purposely exposing the secret because you want to leave the clan?"

"No. Of course not. I would never purposely expose any of you. But I don't want to propagate the clan. I've only been with Ruby a short time, but I want to try to make a life with her. She knows what I am and accepts me. Isn't that what we all wish for? To find someone who loves you for who you are? Whether it's a Sasquatch mate or another?"

Voices murmured throughout the chapel. Joe banged his gavel on the table.

"Quiet. Mating out of species is contradictive to the overall good and will not be tolerated."

"Just because something has been the way it is all these years, doesn't mean it's the right way or the only way. Are we so xenophobic we're willing to sacrifice the happiness of our people? I know I'm not the only one who feels this way. I'm not saying my choice is the choice you have to make. In fact, I think each of you should be free to choose who you love, regardless of your birth species, human or Sasquatch. That's all I'm really asking for here. How much longer do you think we can hide the clan? I'm not saying we need to come out completely, but wouldn't it be better in the long run if we controlled the story? There will be haters. No matter what you decide. But how does my decision to live my life free of this affliction hurt you?"

"Every Sasquatch life matters," Joe said, angrily.

"Every life matters, period," Ethan retorted.

Voices grumbled low in front of him. The nodding of a few heads encouraged him.

"I know change is hard. And it doesn't all have to happen tonight. But this could be a start for anyone who wants one. The Lummi and other nations have protected us since the beginning. But times change. Species evolve. Maybe it's time we did, too. And we can't evolve if we fall back into the same old ways because we're afraid to change." Ethan turned and pointed to Joe. "He wants me to make a match. With

Elizabeth. I don't love Elizabeth." Ethan shot her an apologetic look. "Hell, I've only just met Ruby. But she's amazing and kind and open, and I'd like the chance to see where that could lead. You know? Like regular people. I know what Jacob and I did may seem extreme. Traitorous, even, as Joseph has already said. You have my word, no other Sasquatches will be exposed unless they choose to come forward themselves. The world will have plenty to digest with the knowledge they already have and will gain from us. Each of you is free to choose your path. This is the path for me."

He looked at Ruby. Tears filled her eyes and leaked out the sides. Claire clutched her hand.

The low rumble of voices became a din as Lummi and Sasquatch debated the merits and perils of coming out to the world.

Joe banged his gavel until the noise slackened. He swept his angry gaze across the room then closed his eyes briefly. "Unfortunately, we don't have the luxury of time to debate these events. Ethan and Jacob have pressed us into an untenable decision. Yet, we have to make one. It's my thought we should say nothing for now, other than they were members of the tribe. We could deny we knew about their nature or confess we have protected them. I think the only fair way to decide that is to vote by show of hands. No abstaining or anonymity for this vote. You have to take a stand before us all because this vote will decide our path forward." Joe wiped his nose, the emotion of the moment nearly overcoming him. "Those in favor of deniability of their nature, raise your hand."

A few dozen hands rose tentatively into the air then a handful retreated. Joe counted. "Twenty-eight for denial. Those in favor of confessing we've knowingly protected and harbored Ethan and Jacob as Sasquatches, raise your hands."

More than two hundred and seventy-five hands went up.

Joe's face reddened, but he didn't miss a beat. "The choice has been made. Ethan and Jacob will direct the narrative. No outside interviews with the rest of you for now, please. You're all used to keeping secrets. We can keep this as a tribe for a bit longer. A public relations committee will need to be formed to work with Ethan and Jacob. Do we have any volunteers?"

Six hands went up, including Elizabeth's. Joe looked like he was on the verge of a stroke. He banged his gavel again. "Dismissed."

Epilogue

Ethan stared out the boat's window across the Pacific as the last oranges and purples of a fantastic sunset began to fade on the horizon. The fallout of his decision had actually been better than expected. Getting through the crowd of curious media had been challenging after the tribunal, but so far so good. Ethan was thankful for Jacob's offer to lie low on his boat for a few days. Their agreement with Garrett and Faraday had held. Exclusivity in exchange for his privacy when he asked for it. Same went for Jacob and the entire tribe. The agreement had not pleased the public, but it wasn't long before every outlet picked up Garrett's interviews and Faraday's photos and spread them across the globe. They were viral, baby.

He was sure Faraday and Garrett already had fat paychecks in hand, which was fine with him. His privacy and his future were worth the cost. With Ethan's approval, Faraday had broken his suspicions as to Ethan's pen name. Feeling the revelation was the only way to keep the government from ferreting him away for "experiments," Ethan had agreed to that outing as well. He had, however, made it abundantly clear to Faraday his exclusivity hinged on the man's loyalty, in all things. Faraday had gotten the point and enjoyed the spoils of their uncomfortable alliance.

Ruby's hand snaked around his waist and her heat pressed against his backside, warming him in more ways than one.

"What are you thinking about?" she asked.

"Everything. How lucky I am. How happy I am you agreed to hang out with me while we work through this craziness."

"I'm the lucky one. You could have turned out to be a serial killer."

Ethan laughed. "Right. And a Sasquatch is better?"

Ruby slid around in front of him, her hands stroking his increasingly furry cheek and jaw. "You're much more than just a Sasquatch."

He laughed again. "I never thought I'd meet anyone who was okay with me being 'just a Sasquatch.'"

"Ethan, you're not a monster."

"Then what am I?"

"Mine."

Ruby stood on tiptoe and reached around the back of his neck, bringing his face down to hers. She pressed her lips to his, and his mouth opened into a hungry kiss. The boat rocked over a large wave and set them off-balance. Ethan's hands braced on either side of her body against the window behind them and his knee slid between her thighs, brushing against her sex.

His kisses became more urgent, and a growl rumbled low in his chest, which spiked her heartbeat. She broke the kiss and tilted her head back, exposing her throat to him in an animalistic and submissive way she instinctually knew he couldn't resist. Ethan took advantage of her offer and worked his way down her throat, his scruffy beard sparking her desire all the more.

His hands brushed beneath her shirt, setting her torso on fire, and slid up to her breasts. Ethan cupped a breast in each hand, rolling her nipples with his thumbs then reached around to work his oversized T-shirt up and over her head. He lowered his mouth to suckle at her right breast while his other hand slid down the front of her panties and cupped her sex. Ethan's fingers parted her slick folds and a moan escaped her.

The boat rocked again, and Ethan braced them with his shoulder against the window briefly. He slipped his fingers into her channel and filled her, but not enough. Not nearly enough.

Ruby frantically worked to relieve Ethan of his shirt and jeans. He broke free to give her an assist.

"In a hurry?" he asked, a sly smile curling the corner of his mouth.

"Yes," she whispered.

Finally unclothed, she gripped his hips, and her thumbs followed the groove on either side of his abdomen down, down, down to his erection. She grasped him firmly, and his head rocked back in a gasp. He grabbed the brass bar above the window with both hands as Ruby squatted on her heels and took his rock-hard erection into her mouth.

Increasing her suction, she worked her mouth down his cock, rocking with the surge of the boat over and over for several long minutes. Retreating, she teased and nipped along his shaft, licking the underside of his length while she tugged gently at his balls. His thighs tensed, and the skin around his sac wrinkled and tightened beneath her touch. He wasn't going to last much longer.

Rising, she reached up to pull his hand from the brass rail and led him to the bed. Ethan took control and pushed her back onto the bed, grasping her knees to spread her wide before him. He lowered his face to her core and stroked his tongue up and between her folds. Ruby clutched at the comforter for purchase and balled the material tightly in her fists as tension coiled inside her.

Ethan crawled up her body, skin to skin, his warmth engulfing her as her hips rose to meet him. White-hot desire shot to her core when the head of his erection brushed past her folds and paused at her entrance. The slight pressure there was nearly too much to bear. Her body demanded to be filled. Her hips shifted slightly and she pushed against him, gripping his ass and wrapping her heels behind his thighs to pull him into her.

He held back, still teasing at her entrance. "Ethan! Stop teasing me! Get inside me now!"

He chuckled then plunged into her. Stars exploded behind his closed eyelids as he found a rhythm that matched the rocking of the boat. He shifted slightly, and her orgasm uncoiled, ricocheting through her body. She rode the wave and then Ethan stiffened above her as he filled her with his own release.

He collapsed on top of her, crushing her into the soft mattress for a few seconds before he rolled to her right and pulled her against him, spooning her so they could look out on the sea.

They lay together, drifting in and out of sleep. This reprieve wouldn't last. They'd have to rejoin the real world tomorrow and begin their new life. Together.

That one word. *Together.* Made every decision he'd recently made worthwhile. They had much to sort out. Many more interviews in his future. Jacob was in the same boat. Well, not literally, at least not right this moment. Jacob was currently giving medical lectures to a small group of scientists and government officials on the anatomy and biology of their condition. The magic of it all was a bit trickier to explain. Ethan's agent had texted him that book sales had skyrocketed. Suddenly, everyone was reading and rereading his stories with a new eye. His next book was already forming in his head. He was finally free. Free to live his life. Free to write without fear. Free to love whomever he wanted.

He squeezed Ruby tighter.

Ruby snuggled in but stared ahead, out the window. "Do you think there are other mythical creatures out there? Waiting to be revealed?"

"You mean like Cthulhu?" he teased then considered her question for a long moment. "Maybe. Lovecraft says, 'A time will come…' I guess we'll have to deal with one monster rising at a time."

She turned to smile at him, her hand brushing his hair from his forehead as an idea formed. Her other hand reached down to grip his length again. "Speaking of rising…"

 # The End #

Credits & Bibliography

HP Lovecraft: The Complete Fiction by HP Lovecraft
BIGFOOT: The Science, Sightings and Search for America's Elusive Legend *Special NEWSWEEK Edition*
Sasquatch: Legend Meets Science by Jeff Meldrum
Bigfoot Field Research Organization website and reports http://www.bfro.net/
Craigslist for the story inspiration

About the Author

Lisa adores beasties of all sorts, fictional as well as real, and has a farm full of them in her Southwest Missouri home, including: one child, one husband, two dogs, two cats, a dozen hens, thousands of Italian bees and a guinea pig.

She may or may not keep a complete zombie apocalypse bug-out bag in her trunk at all times, including a machete. Just. In. Case.

Keep in touch here:
Website | Facebook | Twitter | Goodreads | Google+ | Pinterest

Don't miss a thing! Sign up for my newsletter http://eepurl.com/9Zhcz

Other Books by Lisa Medley
Haunt My Heart *A Civil War ghost in the 21st century.*
Space Cowboys & Indians (Cosmic Cowboys-Episode 2) *Sexy sci-fi adventure*
The Astronaut's Princess (Cosmic Cowboys-Episode 2) *Sexy sci-fi adventure*
Shifted in Seattle *A sexy Sasquatch story*

Reap & Repent (Book I of The Reaper Series)

Reap & Redeem (Book II of The Reaper Series)
Reap & Reveal (Book III of The Reaper Series)
Reap & Reckon (Book IV of The Reaper Series) - coming soon

The Reaper Series

The only thing worse than having nothing to live for…is having everything to live for.

A small group of reapers and supernatural beings in Meridian, Arkansas are all that stand between humanity and the apocalypse when a fallen angel stages a demonic invasion. In their battle to save the world, each will meet his or her match, discovering the power of love…and the importance of risking everything to protect it.

Made in the USA
Columbia, SC
11 August 2019